Nick knew he had to ask Elaina tonight. Two years had passed, more than enough time for him to fulfill his vow.

Moonlight shone in her eyes, tiny flecks of gold in all that impossible blue. He imagined touching her cheek, her hair, the delicate column of her neck.

Nick frowned. If he lost himself in lust, in the heat she made him feel, this proposal would be even more difficult.

"Elaina, you know that my brother asked me to take care of Lexie, to teach her about being Comanche. But before he died, he talked to me about you, too. He wanted me to protect you." Pausing to breathe, he let the words settle. "The way a Comanche brother would have done in another century."

Her voice quavered. "I don't understand."

Yes, you do, he thought. Deep down you do. You know what a Comanche marriage exchange means.

"I'm proposing, Elaina. In the name of my brother, I'm asking you to marry me."

SHERI WHITEFEATHER

Comanche Vow

Silhouette Books

Published by Silhouette Books

America's Publisher of Contemporary Romance

ISBN-13: 978-0-373-19895-5
ISBN-10:   0-373-19895-7

COMANCHE VOW

SHERI WHITEFEATHER

Sheri WhiteFeather lives in a cowboy community in Central Valley, California. She loves being a writer and credits her husband, Dru, a tribally enrolled member of the Muscogee Creek Nation, for inspiring many of her stories.

Sheri and Dru have two beautiful grown children, a trio of cats and a border collie/queensland heeler that will jump straight into your arms.

Sheri's hobbies include decorating with antiques and shopping in thrift stores for jackets from the sixties and seventies, items that mark her interest in vintage Western wear and hippie fringe.

To contact Sheri, learn more about her books and see pictures of her family, visit her Web site at www.sheriwhitefeather.com.

To my sister, Elaine McCullogh.
I wished we lived closer. We're not twins,
but we could be. To my agent, Irene Goodman,
because you loved the premise of this story.
To my editor, Melissa Jeglinski, because every author
should be so lucky. And to the community members on
eHarlequin.com—thanks for the message board chats.

One

Nick Bluestone waited at the airport, trying not to pace. He had four weeks to enforce his plan, the mission he'd agreed to carry out.

The mission? Nick frowned. This wasn't a covert military operation. This was a heart-wrenching promise he'd made to his brother. A Comanche vow.

He took a rough breath and thought about Elaina, the woman he'd pledged to marry. He hadn't seen her since the summer they'd buried Grant, the summer they'd stood side by side and mourned Nick's twin. And now, two years later, she had finally agreed to visit him in Oklahoma, to bring his niece for Christmas.

Nick released the air in his lungs. A holiday visit. That wasn't the half of it. Elaina had no idea that he intended to propose. But then, how could she? He'd been keeping the vow a secret, preparing himself for the right moment to tell her.

Scanning the passengers entering the terminal, he spotted her. Instantly his pulse quickened. He barely knew Elaina. Sure, he liked her, but he hadn't allowed himself to look too closely, to admire her for anything other than being his brother's devoted wife.

But damn it, there she was, tall and shapely, with a shoulder-length sweep of chestnut hair—a woman much too striking not to notice.

Even dressed in blue jeans, she reminded him of a lady, a true lady, the sort a noble knight would lose his heart to. Was that what had first attracted Grant to her? The graceful beauty? The whisper of sensuality?

I'm supposed to protect my brother's ladylove, he thought nervously. Pledge my life, my tarnished honor to her. And seeing Elaina, watching her enter his rough-hewn world, made that vow seem more real.

More intense.

Shifting his focus, Nick schooled his anxiety and studied his twelve-year-old niece instead. Lexie was taller than the last time he'd seen her, but still small for her age. A baseball cap rode low on her forehead, shading big, dark eyes. With her baggy jeans and oversize T-shirt, she looked more like a brooding little boy than a troubled young girl.

She glanced up, and he smiled. Her face was lean and angular, her skin smooth and soft. Oh, yeah, he thought.

She was female, all right. Sweet, stubborn and confusing as hell.

He moved forward to greet her, keeping Elaina in his peripheral vision. "Hey, Lexie."

"Uncle Nick."

She reached out, and he hugged her naturally. Lexie was his godchild, the little girl who lived in his heart. She was all he had left of Grant, and he intended to keep her safe and warm.

He lifted the brim of her hat and grinned. Her hair, nearly as short as his, brushed her neck in a simple, blunt style. Apparently Lexie still didn't fuss or frill over her hair, a fact that used to amuse her daddy. No ribbons and bows for Grant's baby girl. She preferred baseball cards to Barbie dolls and barrettes.

And then there was Elaina, rife with feminine curves, in a champagne-colored sweater, slim-fitting jeans and a pair of sleek suede boots. And her eyes, he thought. They were as blue as the brightest lapis imaginable.

Elaina Bluestone.

Ironically, the name fit. Something he'd never noticed before.

"Hi," Nick said to her. "How was your flight?"

"Fine. A little tiring." She met his gaze, and then shifted those blue eyes quickly away. "We had a layover in Texas."

"Yeah. Traveling can wear a person out." Since they didn't embrace, he relieved her of a carry-on bag and tried to act casual. Apparently she didn't like looking him in the eye, but he figured his resemblance to Grant unnerved her. These days, it unnerved him, too. "Let's head over to baggage claim."

They stood quietly with the other passengers and waited for the luggage to appear. And while Lexie adjusted her backpack and Elaina studied the empty turntable, Nick's thoughts drifted back in time.

Two years before, he'd visited Grant in Los Angeles, a trip he rarely made. The Comanche brothers looked alike, but their lifestyles had been worlds apart. Grant had left home to pursue a successful corporate career in California, while Nick, a saddle maker, remained close to his roots.

So to celebrate Nick's last night in the city, they'd eaten dinner at a steak house, then stopped by a sports bar to shoot a few rounds of pool. Although neither had consumed more than a few beers, they were still feeling boyish and rowdy, ribbing each other like a couple of kids.

"You miss this shot," Nick had cajoled, "and I get to take that jet-propelled machine of yours for a spin. You know, the one masquerading as a car."

Grant had flashed a roguish grin and eyed the eight ball, calling it in the corner pocket. "Then I don't intend to miss, bro. Because I've seen the way you drive."

He didn't miss, and Nick didn't end up piloting the Porsche. It was Grant who had driven later that night, Grant who had been gunned down in the midst of a carjacking.

As a familiar pain coiled in the pit of his stomach, Nick squinted at the baggage-claim ticket in Elaina's hand.

He could still recall that moment, the instant his brother lay dying in his arms. He'd struggled to stem the wound, to stop the warm rush of blood that had flowed from Grant's chest.

A part of him knew he couldn't help the other man, but another part refused to give up. He couldn't live without his brother. In spite of the choices that separated them, they still shared the same heart, the same soul. There were times they could read each other's minds, feel each other's emotions.

And on that dark summer night, Nick had felt his twin die. But not before Grant had whispered the words Nick would never forget.

"Take care of my family...the old way. Be the Comanche I should have been. Teach my daughter... protect my wife...."

The old way. A dying man's last request. A living man's biggest fear. Grant had asked Nick to take his place—become a husband and father to the woman and child he'd left behind.

"It's here."

Nick blinked at the sound of Elaina's voice. "What?"

"Our luggage."

"Oh, sure. Just tell me which suitcases are yours."

He squared his shoulders, his thoughts still spinning.

Marrying Elaina and raising Lexie was a responsibility he'd been battling for two years.

He lifted a leather satchel, wondering about the path that lay ahead. Would Elaina actually agree to marry him? And what about his involvement in Grant's death? She didn't know about the mistake Nick had made, the vital error that had ultimately cost Grant his life.

No one knew. Not even the L.A. cops who'd taken the report. Nick still kept the truth locked inside, the pain and guilt that followed him each day.

Nick's house was one of those quaint country structures with an enormous porch, a graveled driveway and grass and trees everywhere. It was more or less what Elaina had expected, a little off the beaten path, with neighbors scattered here and there.

"Your dad and I grew up on this property," Nick told Lexie as he unlocked the door. "But I tore down the old house and built a new one. It was pretty primitive before."

Lexie only nodded. After hugging Nick at the airport, she'd withdrawn, reverting back to her detached self.

He carried the heavier luggage inside, with Elaina and Lexie carting smaller pieces.

"You brought a lot of stuff," he commented.

"Four weeks is a lengthy vacation," Elaina responded, worrying about what she'd gotten herself into. Lexie didn't look any happier, even if she kept studying her uncle beneath her lashes.

Grant's senseless murder had destroyed Lexie, each year going from bad to worse. And to top it off, her best friend had moved three months ago, leaving the young girl feeling lost and lonely. Elaina sighed. She was an elementary-school teacher, a woman experienced in meeting the needs of a wide range of children, yet she couldn't help her own daughter. How ironic was that?

She had even taken a leave of absence from her job, but being a stay-at-home mom hadn't made a difference. Then again, Lexie appeared to be craving a paternal-type attachment. Which was the reason Elaina had finally agreed to come to Oklahoma. Recently, Lexie had expressed an interest in visiting her uncle.

Elaina studied Nick, wondering what sort of person he really was. She didn't know much about him. In truth, he'd always seemed a little wild—a man with a rough, frayed-denim edge.

She hoped they weren't going to spend the next four weeks struggling to make conversation. Whenever Nick had visited them in L.A., Grant had been the one entertaining his brother. Aside from the days following Grant's death, this was the first time Elaina or Lexie had ever been alone with Nick.

But Elaina had to give him credit for trying. He'd invited them to stay with him during summer and spring breaks, and since those attempts had failed, he'd resorted to Christmas.

He showed them to their rooms, and then motioned

to the burgers they'd picked up at a drive-through on the way in. "Ready for dinner?" he asked.

She nodded. "Sure."

"We can eat in here," he said, indicating the living room. "I'm not fussy about stuff like that. But I guess that's pretty obvious."

Both Elaina and Lexie managed a smile. Remnants from Nick's last meal sat on a plate above the television, as if he'd forgotten about it until now.

As they gathered around the coffee table, sipping sodas and dipping fries into pools of ketchup, Elaina assessed her surroundings.

The room was rough-hewn and masculine, with coarse furnishings and an Old West theme. A set of buckhorn candleholders sat on a sturdy oak bookcase, and a rope-and-rawhide chair was angled in the corner. A lambskin throw decorated the sofa, along with a few Western-printed pillows.

The end table was a bit cluttered, newspapers and magazines piled in an uneven stack. Elaina had the urge to tidy up. It was her nature, she supposed, the domestic side of herself she couldn't deny.

Glancing out the window, she caught sight of a country setting, of dusk darkening a winter sky.

Grant and Nick had grown up on this rugged property, but Nick accepted it as his home. The man was a saddle maker, an Indian living like a cowboy. Grant had preferred designer suits, whereas Nick appeared to favor worn-out Wranglers. How could they look so much alike, yet be so different from each other?

Elaina reached for her burger, wishing Nick didn't have Grant's face. Here she was, two years after her husband's death, comparing the brothers and imagining Grant as he had been.

She knew Lexie did that, too. And Nick, with his jet-black hair, determined jaw and strong cheekbones, was a reminder of what they had lost.

Was coming here a mistake? she asked herself. Was Lexie placing too much importance on her father's twin?

Nick turned on the TV, and Elaina let out the breath she'd been holding. Hopefully, she and Lexie would get through this evening painlessly, watching cable for a while, then retreating to unpack and get a much-needed night's rest.

The following morning Elaina awakened feeling far from refreshed. She squinted at the clock and reached for her robe. They day seemed a little gray, but she supposed it matched her mood.

Oklahoma. Grant hadn't liked living here, so what made her think four weeks in the Sooner State was going to cure Lexie's depression?

Concerned about her daughter, she belted her robe and slipped into the hall. Opening the other guest-room door, she stepped inside, then stood near the bed.

Lexie slept in a tangle of blankets, her short black

hair strewn across her face. She had Grant's hair, rain straight, with a glossy sheen. Elaina's unruly mane tended to curl far too much. If she didn't style it with a blow dryer, each rebellious strand took on a mind of its own.

Lexie stirred, and Elaina sighed. Should she wake the young girl or let her sleep?

She touched her daughter's cheek. She missed the closeness they'd once shared, the laughter that used to fill their home.

Three teenage boys had destroyed her family. They'd wanted Grant's car badly enough to kill him for it, to shoot him in the chest and leave him bleeding on the side of the freeway.

She took a deep breath, but the image wouldn't go away. Her husband shivering and helpless, a bullet lodged much too close to his heart. And what about Nick? She would never forget how he looked when a policeman brought him back to the condo that night. Her husband was dead, and his twin had blood on his sleeve, a tremor in his voice, a vacant stare in his dark eyes.

"Mom?"

Elaina's heart bumped against her breast, jarring her from the memory. "Hi, sweetheart."

Lexie adjusted the covers. "What time is it?"

"Seven."

"Are we going somewhere with Uncle Nick?"

She sat on the edge of the bed. "Not that I know of.

He's probably working today." Which meant he would still be close by. His workshop was located behind the house.

"Then can I go back to sleep?"

Elaina considered her daughter's question. This was supposed to be a vacation, four weeks away from the pattern of their lives. There was no dreaded middle school for Lexie to tackle, no unhappy morning routine to adhere to. So if Lexie wanted to stay in bed, what was the harm? She was probably overtired, her body still trying to adjust to the time change.

"I'll wake you up later, okay?"

"Okay."

Lexie closed her eyes, big brown eyes that nearly swallowed her entire face. She was, Elaina thought, a petite and pretty tomboy, caught in the battle of puberty. An unwelcome battle, considering Lexie's determination to defy her gender.

Elaina went back to her own room, choosing to wear jeans, a washable-silk T-shirt and a pair of lace-up boots. She styled her hair in a classic chignon, a look she had become accustomed to, even with casual clothes.

Ready for a cup of coffee, she headed for the kitchen, preparing to familiarize herself with someone else's home. But when she got there, she came eye-to-eye with Nick.

He leaned against the counter, his raven hair combed away from his face, a well-worn denim shirt tucked into a pair of equally faded jeans. She had to tell herself to breathe, to accept his presence without losing her composure.

It was his hair, she realized, that unsettled her most. Nick had always kept it long, well past his shoulders. Yet the morning after Grant had died, he'd cut it.

But why? So he would look even more like his brother?

Grant had worn his hair in a shorter style because he was trying to present a non-Indian image. He'd wanted people to see him as the up-and-coming executive that he was. And stereotypes, he'd said, referring to his Comanche heritage, got in the way.

"Good morning," Nick drawled in a slow, husky voice. "Did you sleep all right?"

"Yes. Thank you." Unlike Grant, he was heavily involved in his culture, or that was the impression she got. He sported silver jewelry, a wide band on one wrist, a detailed watch and another wide bracelet on the other. His belt was adorned with sterling accents and an engraved buckle.

No one would mistake Nick for being anything other than Indian, and his denim-and-silver style intensified that image. Except for the hair. The slicked-back, *GQ* look belonged to Grant.

"Where's Lexie?" he asked.

"Still asleep."

"Oh." He frowned. "I was wondering what everyone wanted to do about breakfast."

"I'd rather wait for Lexie, but I'm not going to wake her for a while. So if you want to eat now, go ahead."

"No. I can wait."

She noticed the coffeepot was percolating. "May I have a cup?"

"Sure. It's pretty strong, though."

"I don't mind." Elaina wasn't choosy about her coffee, and she'd lied about sleeping well. She'd tossed and turned most of the night. Of course, insomnia had become part of her widowed lifestyle.

She located a sturdy mug in the cupboard above her head, then turned back to him. "Do you have sugar?"

"Oh, yeah. Sorry." He opened the cabinet near the stove and handed her a pink-and-white box.

She added the sweetener and found herself smiling in the process. This was typical of a bachelor, she supposed. A sugar bowl wouldn't occur to a single man. And that's what Nick had always been. Her bachelor brother-in-law.

She lifted the mug, curious if Nick had a significant other by now, an important girlfriend who kept him in line. Not likely, she thought. Hadn't she stumbled upon a conversation between Grant and Nick on that very subject, just days before Grant's murder?

"So, bro," her husband had said, sinking into an Italian leather chair. "Have you met anyone special?"

Nick, looking a bit too rugged for the condo's upscale interior, had kicked a pair of timeworn boots out in front of him. "Can't say that I have."

"I guess that means you're still sampling the flavor of the month?"

"Yep. That's me. Brunettes in May and redheads in June." Nick had wagged his eyebrows, and they'd grinned at each other like a couple of naughty boys paging through their first girlie magazine. Elaina had wanted to throttle both of them, but instead she'd tossed a decorative pillow at Grant, warning him that she'd just entered the living room.

And even though Grant had charmed her into a playful, I'm-busted hug, and Nick had seemed thoroughly embarrassed that she'd heard his macho admission, that silly memory confirmed the unlikelihood of a significant other. Nick Bluestone wasn't the commitment type.

"Elaina?"

She glanced up and realized he'd been watching her, probably wondering why she had zoned out. "Yes?"

He trapped her gaze, his stare intense. "Do you want to go for a walk? Maybe help feed the horses?"

With a sudden jump in her heartbeat, she told herself to relax, to not look away. She couldn't continue to avoid him, and dancing around those dark, penetrating eyes was simply rude.

"Do you think I need a jacket?" she asked, deciding to walk with him.

"Maybe. I don't think it's cold out, but you might." He sent her a boyish grin. "You've got that California blood."

And he had a charming smile, a bit more crooked than Grant's had been. "I'll get a sweater." She went to her room and returned with a lightweight wrap. She'd meant to smile back at him, but she couldn't. Her attraction to Grant had started with his teasing grin.

The air was brisk and clean, with mountains in the distance. They passed Nick's workshop and headed toward the barn. She noticed a fenced arena and a small, circular pen. Equestrian additions, she assumed, Nick had made to the property. Grant had described his childhood homestead as a wasteland, but Elaina thought it was pretty. The soil shimmered with flecks of gold, and a cluster of trees was shedding winter leaves. She could picture snow blanketing the earth, just enough to make the holidays come alive.

"Do you ride?" Nick asked.

"I used to rent horses in the Hollywood Hills, but it's been ages. Since high school, I guess."

"Somehow I can't see connecting with nature in Hollywood. That place is weird."

Elaina had to laugh. He sounded like a big, biased country boy. "It was near Griffith Park, so it's nice up there. But I suppose your opinion of Tinseltown is accurate enough. Some people call it Holly*weird*."

This time he laughed, a rich, smooth baritone. She liked the friendly sound, but when he leaned closer and bumped her shoulder, her heart picked up speed. A slice of hair fell across his forehead, and she realized it wasn't secured with gel. Nick's hair was simply wet from a recent shower and drying naturally in the morning air.

Suddenly she couldn't stop herself from asking the question that had plagued her for two years.

"Nick?" She stopped walking and turned to face him. "Why did you cut your hair?"

He stared at her for a moment. "Because of Grant," he said quietly.

She released a shaky breath. "Because that's the way he wore his hair?"

"No. It's a Comanche practice." His eyes turned a darker shade of brown—a deeper, lonelier color. "My brother died. I'm mourning him."

Elaina felt instantly shamed. She should have figured it out on her own. She should have known. Hadn't she seen something similar in movies? Indians maiming themselves when a loved one died—cutting their skin, their hair? She looked at Nick and wondered if he'd taken a knife to himself, as well. If there were scars somewhere on his body.

"Does it help?" she asked. "Does it take the pain away?"

He closed his eyes, and as the wind blew around him in a silent flutter, Elaina waited for him to answer.

But he didn't. He just stood, with his eyes closed. Stood while her heart pounded in an unsteady rhythm.

"Nick?" she pressed. If there was a way to ease the pain that came with losing Grant, then Elaina needed to know.

Two

Nick didn't know what to say. Nothing helped, nothing made living without his brother more bearable. Yes, he'd cut his hair, honoring the old way, but keeping it short was more than a mourning ritual. It was a daily reminder of what he'd done, of his involvement in Grant's death. And so were the marks on his chest, the places where he'd shed his own blood. The wounds had long since healed, but the pain and guilt wouldn't go away.

He opened his eyes and gazed at Elaina. She watched him, her heart on her sleeve. She was hurting, too. Trying to find a way to cope with being a widow, with raising a troubled daughter.

"No," he said. "It doesn't help. But it's part of my

culture. And I've always followed the early practices. The best I can, anyway. Sometimes it's difficult living in modern times and adhering to the old ways."

Elaina tilted her head. "Grant was concerned about being stereotyped, but other than that, he rarely talked about being Indian. It didn't seem to be a major issue in his life."

But it was, Nick thought. Grant had turned away from their heritage long ago. Yet on that dark summer night, he'd come back to his roots. He'd died in Nick's arms, asking Nick to take his place the way a Comanche brother would have done centuries before.

He looked at Elaina, knowing how much Grant had loved her. And now it was Nick's responsibility to keep her happy and safe, to provide for her well-being.

She was pretty. Nick couldn't deny how soft her skin seemed or how daylight played upon her hair, intensifying subtle copper hues. What man wouldn't find her attractive? She had long, lean curves, the kind of body that made a pair of blue jeans seem sleek yet sinful.

Was he supposed to sleep with her? Make love to her on their wedding night?

Nick jammed his hands in his pockets. Of course he was. Sex was part of the marriage tradition. A natural, normal, healthy physical release.

And one that made him nervous as hell. Elaina was his brother's wife, the woman Grant had loved.

"Are you all right?" she asked, placing her hand on his shoulder.

"Yeah. I'm fine. I just miss my brother."

"Me, too."

They stood in the middle of the yard, their gazes locked, the morning air scented with horses and hay. A loose strand of Elaina's hair blew around her face, breaking free from the ladylike confinement.

Her eyes were so blue, so emotional, that Nick wanted to kiss her.

He wanted to kiss his brother's wife.

Because the thought confused him, he stepped back. She was beautiful, and Grant had asked him to take care of her, but somehow she still seemed forbidden. A woman who was his, yet wasn't.

He resumed walking. "We better get the horses watered and fed."

She stayed beside him. "Just tell me what to do."

They reached the barn, and he led her to the feed room. While loading a wheelbarrow, he explained that he kept a stockpile of hay for colder months.

"It doesn't seem like winter," she commented. "I was hoping for a little snow. You know, just enough to play in."

He had to smile. A California girl imagining a white Christmas. "It might happen. Will Rogers used to say that if you don't like the weather in Oklahoma, wait a minute and it'll change."

She chuckled, and he glanced up from his task. A few more strands of her hair had come loose. He had the notion to brush it away from her cheek, but proceeded to section the hay instead. He supposed the pinned-up style was her teacher hairdo—proper and pretty.

They approached the box stalls, and Elaina made a beeline for Nick's moodiest mount, a gray he called Kid. The gelding tossed his head and stepped back warily, even if his breakfast was within sniffing distance.

"What's the matter?" she asked the horse in a soft voice. "Are you bashful?"

Kid was more than head-shy. The three-year-old had acquired every leave-me-alone habit Nick could think of. "That's Kid. I haven't had him for very long. He's a bit of a project."

"You're going to work with him?"

"Yeah." And this was Nick's first attempt to make a gentleman out of an ill-mannered mount. "I'm a saddle maker, not a trainer, but I've got plenty of patience."

Elaina stepped back to view the horse. "I like him."

"Really?" Surprised, Nick entered the stall and pushed against the gelding's rump when Kid tried to crowd him. They went through the same routine every morning. Kid was determined to jam Nick against the wall, and Nick was determined to make the horse behave. "Besides the fact that his stall manners are deplorable, he bites, kicks and pulls away while he's being led. Oh, and he charges in pasture, too."

Kid pinned his ears, and Elaina managed an amused look. "You must like him, too. After all, you did buy him."

"He was cheap." And Kid's previous owners had

given up on the feisty gelding, the way Nick's mom had given up on him and Grant. She'd walked away, leaving behind a shabby old house and two confused boys.

He exited Kid's stall and received a good-riddance sneer on his way out.

Elaina stifled a laugh. "He's trying so hard to be a tough guy."

"Yeah, well, he's a pain in the ass." Nick reached into the wheelbarrow and filled Kid's hay crib. "And if he doesn't shape up, he's going to end up as some spoiled little poodle's dinner." He sent the gelding a pointed look. "They make dog food out of rotten horses, you know."

Kid sneered again, and Elaina gave in to the urge to laugh. Nick turned to watch her, to see the light dancing in those incredible blue eyes.

"His name certainly suits him," she said. "Every kid I know makes that face at one time or another."

"Even Lexie?"

Her laughter faded. "Especially Lexie."

They stood in silence then, looking at each other. Her breath hitched, and he ignored complaints from a row of hungry horses. Nick didn't know what it felt like to be a parent, but he knew how it felt to honor his dying brother's last request, to promise to devote the rest of his life to Grant's family.

"Lexie's really sad, isn't she?"

Elaina nodded. "Sad, angry, confused. Her father was murdered, her best friend moved and she's battling puberty. That's enough to send anyone over the edge."

"I guess you've gone the doctor route," he said, feeling useless.

In an absent gesture, she lifted a blade of hay. "Yes, but Lexie wasn't very receptive to therapy. Antidepressants didn't help, either."

Nick frowned. "They gave her drugs? That sounds so severe."

"Antidepressants work for some people, but Lexie experienced too many side effects." She dropped the hay, watched it drift to the ground. "I guess it was too much to hope for. A pill that would make her happy."

"Yeah. That doesn't sound realistic." And the idea that a twelve-year-old needed a happy pill made his heart ache.

Maybe it was time to talk to Lexie, to tell her that she had been in her father's thoughts before he died.

"I'm going to help you with Lexie," Nick said. "Whatever I can do."

Her smile was soft, her voice a little broken. "Thank you."

"Sure. No problem." Feeling suddenly awkward, he reached for the wheelbarrow, sucked in a rough breath. "I guess we better get these animals fed."

"I'll fill the water buckets."

She turned away, and he let out the breath he'd been holding.

So what about Elaina? When should he tell her about their pending marriage? Today? Tomorrow? Next week?

Take care of my family...the old way. Be the Comanche I should have been. Teach my daughter... protect my wife.

Your wife. Dear God, brother, you gave me your wife. The woman you held in your arms every night.

I can't tell her today, Nick thought, catching sight of Elaina's hair shimmering in the morning light. He could tackle only one obstacle at a time. And for now, he had a twelve-year-old girl to worry about.

Twenty minutes later, Nick and Elaina stood in the kitchen, discussing breakfast.

"We can have something here," he said. "Unless you want to go out."

"Here is fine."

He opened the fridge. "I've got bacon and eggs." Food he'd purchased with Elaina and Lexie in mind. Normally he started his day with a bowl of cereal and two cups of black coffee. "I'm not a great cook," he admitted.

She turned to wash her hands. "I don't mind fixing breakfast."

"All right. Thanks." He shifted his feet, feeling uncomfortable in his own kitchen. Nick wasn't used to company, to having to consider someone else's preference.

He pulled a hand through his shorn hair. This husband thing was going to take some adjustment.

"Are the pans in here?" she asked, pointing to the cabinet below the stove.

"Yeah." He placed a carton of eggs and a pound of bacon on the counter, and found himself looking around, wondering if his house was too simple for Elaina. He'd designed the kitchen for practicality, but it wasn't fancy. And neither was the rest of the place. The decor was sturdy, woodsy and Western. A far cry, he thought, from her city-slick condo with its creamy carpet and floor-to-ceiling windows.

Elaina set a pan on the stove. "Maybe I should wake Lexie first."

"I can do that." And it would give him an opportunity to talk to his niece in private. "I'd like to spend a few minutes alone with her."

"That's nice." Elaina smiled. "She'd probably like that, too."

"Okay. Good. Just call us when breakfast is ready."

"No problem," she responded, still smiling a little.

Elaina had a pretty smile, he thought as he turned and headed down the hall. A sexy mouth. Which, of course, wasn't what a marriage was based on. Sometimes Nick wanted to forget the whole thing, convince himself that Grant had been in shock and didn't know what he was saying.

But deep in his heart he knew that wasn't true. Hadn't they talked about it when they were kids? He could still hear their voices, two sixth-grade boys discussing their heritage, a year after their mother had left.

"All that old Comanche stuff is weird," Grant had said.

"No, it's not. I think it's kinda cool that a man got to have more than one wife."

"You would, Nicky. You're a pervert."

They both laughed. Nick had already kissed a girl. Not a wet kiss, but a lip lock just the same.

"I wish we could have lived back then," he said, picturing his ancestors riding across the plains. "We would have been awesome warriors."

Grant rolled his eyes. "Yeah, right. I can see it now. You'd die in battle, and I'd end up having to marry all your wives and raise all your goofy kids."

Nick frowned. "I'd do that for you."

"Really?"

"Yeah."

"Okay, but my kids aren't gonna be goofy," Grant said, punching his twin's shoulder. "My kids are gonna be cool."

Nick punched him back, and they laughed again, brothers who loved each other more than anything.

The memory faded, and Nick swallowed the lump in his throat.

He knocked on Lexie's door, waited a beat and heard a muffled, groggy-sounding "It's okay, Mom. I'm awake."

"I'm not your mom. It's Uncle Nick. Can I come in?"

"Yes."

She was sitting up in bed, the blanket bunched around her hips. Her sweats were a standard shade of gray, and her sleepy eyes were the shape of her mother's and the color of her father's. Lexie Bluestone was a youthful combination of Elaina and Grant. Her size was a bit puzzling, though, considering how tall her parents were.

Maybe Elaina had been a late bloomer. Nick didn't know much about his future wife.

His *possible* future wife, he amended. She might not agree to marry him. Asking a white woman to adhere to an old Comanche practice was asking a lot.

"Morning, Lexie," Nick said, his heart hammering in his chest.

"Hi." She reached for a pillow and hugged it.

She looked like a lost soul, a little girl with big, sad eyes. I'm sorry, he thought. So sorry I took your father away.

Nick moved forward, then sat on the edge of the bed. "I was hoping we could talk for a few minutes."

"About what?"

"Your dad."

Lexie's eyes got bigger, and he realized he'd caught her off guard. Smooth move, Bluestone. Just sock her in the gut with it. "There's just something I wanted to tell you."

She hugged the pillow a little tighter. "About my dad?"

Nick nodded. "About the night he died."

"You were there," she said, her hair falling across her face in a sleek black line. "You were with him."

"Your dad talked to me before he died." Although Nick wanted to brush the hair from her cheek, he kept his hands clasped in his lap. "Some of his last words were about you."

Lexie didn't respond. She just watched him with those luminous eyes.

"He asked me to look after you. And to teach you about being Comanche."

She blinked, and he saw a shimmer of tears. "Is that what you're going to do?" she asked.

"Yes, I am. Is that okay with you?"

When she nodded, her chin bumped the pillow. "I guess so. I mean, if that's what my dad wanted."

They both fell silent. The room was still dim, vertical blinds shutting out the morning light. Nick remembered holding Lexie at her christening, a tiny babe draped in white lace. Grant had been so proud.

"Uncle Nick?"

"Yes?" He met her watery gaze, wishing he knew how to comfort her.

"Did you like being a twin?"

He pictured his brother's face. "Sure. I liked it a lot. Your dad was my best friend. Sometimes we could read each other's minds. Or we'd say the same thing at the same time."

"You look so much like him. Even your voices sound

alike. But your hair used to be longer than his, so I guess nobody ever mixed you up."

"We both had long hair when we were kids." He smiled a little, enjoying the memory. "So you see, people confused us all the time. Especially our teachers. Of course, we drove them crazy on purpose. Twins get to play all kinds of games in school."

Lexie drew her knees up, a child keen with interest. "What about your mom? Could she tell you apart?"

"Yeah, she knew who was who." And she'd left both of them behind. "Did your dad mention her?"

Lexie nodded. "He said that the man she was going to marry was a jerk, so you guys stayed with your grandma instead of going with your mom when she moved."

Nick glanced up at the ceiling. That wasn't exactly the truth, but it was a hell of a lot better than saying their mom had abandoned them. "Our grandma was a great lady."

"Do you have any pictures of her?" she asked, scooting forward a little.

"Sure. I've got a box of old photos. There's some of your dad and me when we were kids, too."

Her eyes were still watery, but she smiled. "Can we look through them later?"

"You bet." Nick knew Grant had left home without any childhood mementos, so Nick had saved pictures and report cards and scraps of paper with adolescent notes scribbled on them. Just in case, he'd always told himself. Just in case Grant stopped being ashamed of who they were and where they'd come from.

Lexie lowered her head. "I wish people didn't have to die. I miss Daddy so much."

"I know, baby. Me, too."

She looked up, her voice quavering. "Do you ever think about the boys who killed him?"

A blast of pain exploded in Nick's chest. When the bullet had struck Grant, he'd fallen, too. He'd dropped to his knees to cradle his twin. "Sometimes."

"Do you still remember what they look like?"

"Yes." He would never forget their faces, teenagers who were monsters deep inside. "I gave the police a description." And he'd spent hours paging through mug shots, studying gangbangers, murders, drug addicts and thieves. "They'll get caught someday."

She adjusted the blanket. "I hope so. It isn't fair that they got away."

He frowned, the impact of her words constricting his heart. "I know." If only he could go back in time, if only there was a way to change what he'd done that night. He reached for Lexie's hand, skimming her fingers with his.

But there was nothing Nick could do but fulfill the promise he'd made to Grant. His brother was gone, and Lexie needed a father.

Three

At nine that evening the wind blew furiously, but inside Nick's house the air was calm and warm. An orange-and-gold flame danced in the fireplace, scenting the living room with a woodsy aroma.

Lexie was perched on the edge of the sofa in youthful anticipation, waiting for Nick. Elaina sat next to her, watching Lexie through the corner of her eye. She hadn't realized how important Grant's deceased relatives would be to her daughter.

Grant hadn't liked talking about his childhood, and Elaina had never pressed the issue. She preferred not to dwell on her childhood, either. And most of her relatives were still alive.

"Here it is." Nick entered the room carrying a cardboard box. He placed it on the coffee table, and Lexie got up and knelt on the floor. Elaina leaned in, too. She couldn't help being curious about her husband's past, about all the things he didn't like to talk about. But then his family had been struggling-to-survive poor, and Grant had valued the finer things in life.

"I meant to put all of this stuff in photo albums," Nick said, removing three vinyl-covered albums. "But I never got around to it." Shoving them aside, he grabbed a stack of loose photos. "Everything's kind of mixed up. We'll just have to sort through it."

"I don't mind." Lexie lifted the picture on top. "Oh. Wow. It's you and Daddy, isn't it?"

He rested his chin on the child's narrow shoulder. "Yep. That's us. Holey jeans and all."

"Who's who?"

He chuckled. "Hell if I know."

"Come on, Uncle Nick." Lexie brought the picture closer. "You have to know."

"Maybe, but I'm not telling."

Lexie rolled her eyes. "Then we'll figure it out. Won't we, Mom?" She handed the photo to Elaina. The teasing banter between uncle and niece surprised her, and so did the snapshot.

Two adolescent boys mugged for the camera, straight black hair falling to their shoulders. Their plaid shirts were frayed, their jeans torn in the same spot, as if they'd skinned the same knee. Elaina examined each face, each identical feature, and when she compared their smiles, she knew. The difference was subtle, barely there, but she still knew. Nick was on the left, his grin just a little more crooked.

"I can't tell," she said, unable to admit the truth. She didn't want Nick to know she had studied him so closely. Besides, it should have been Grant's boyish smile that struck familiarity, not Nick's.

Lexie peered at the photograph again, and Nick flashed the giveaway grin. "Your dad's the cute one," he told his niece.

They were both heartbreakers, Elaina thought. Lean, lanky boys standing in front of a tree they had probably climbed a thousand times.

"Look at this, Mom."

The next snapshot made Elaina's heart thump. It was Grant posing during his early college days. She could see the California campus behind him. The university where they'd met just a few years later.

Nick glanced up, and the moment turned strangely quiet. Firelight played upon his features, making his cheekbones more prominent, his skin a liquid shade of bronze. She actually wanted to touch him, to see if his face would feel as compelling as Grant's.

"My brother thought you were the most beautiful woman on earth."

She blinked, trying to keep herself from crying in front of her daughter. "He told you that?"

"Yeah. He called me after your first date. 'I just

kissed the most gorgeous girl in the world,' he said. 'And someday I'm going to marry her.'"

"And what did you say?" This came from Lexie, her youthful voice surprisingly romantic.

Nick continued to stare at Elaina. "That she must be something special."

Her husband. Her brother-in-law. Their faces were blurring, and it scared her. She needed to remember Grant's features, his smile, his slow, sexy drawl. And she couldn't bear to have Nick watching her with those stirring dark eyes, reminiscing about things that made her ache.

Elaina wanted to run, but there was nowhere to go. She placed the picture back on the table and picked up a different one.

Immediately the image of a young Indian woman caught her attention. Her trendy clothes and retro hairstyle depicted the mod era of the sixties. She sat on a worn-out sofa, a colorful miniskirt revealing shapely legs and chunky-heeled boots. Her eyes were heavily lined and her lipstick a bit too frosted, but she was still stunning.

"Who's this?" Elaina asked, passing the photograph to Nick.

He gazed at it for a moment. "My mom."

Lexie leaned over, bumping Elaina's shoulder. "Wow. She looks like a model or something. How did she make her hair have that little bubble on top?"

Nick shrugged. "I don't know. Lots of hair spray, I guess."

"She's pretty. Isn't she, Mom?"

"Yes, she is." The young woman in the picture was fashionably slim, with a rebellious tilt to her frosted lips. Between the tastefully teased hair, the vinyl go-go boots and the fishnet stockings, Lexie couldn't take her eyes from the photograph.

And neither could Elaina. "She must have gotten a lot of attention." Especially, she thought, in a quiet Oklahoma town.

"Yeah," Nick said. "She always fixed herself up."

His voice sounded a little too casual, a little too unaffected, like the tone of someone feigning nonchalance.

"Now let me see if I can find a picture of Grandma." He scoured the pile, and even though he didn't bury the image of his miniskirted mother, he managed to steer the conversation away from it. "Here she is. Her name was Delores, but most people called her Dee."

Contrary to her striking daughter, whose name Nick had yet to mention, Dee Bluestone exhibited homespun qualities. Her black hair was streaked with gray, her dress an old-fashioned housecoat. And although she smiled for the camera, she seemed tired, aging and overworked.

Now Elaina wanted to know everything Grant hadn't told her. Every detail that had shaped his life, but she wasn't comfortable asking Nick about it.

Nick continued to dig through the pile, handing Lexie his favorite pictures as they surfaced.

"Uncle Nick?"

"Hmm?"

"Can I work on the photo albums?"

"Sure. If you don't mind going through this mess." He retrieved a manila envelope. "There's lots of junk here." He opened the clasp, removed some crumpled papers. "I even saved report cards. Of course, your dad always got better grades than me."

Lexie took the envelope. "Did you go to Indian schools?"

"No. They were public."

The girl turned to Elaina. "Daddy asked Uncle Nick to teach me about being Comanche."

"He did?" Stunned, she glanced at Nick. Grant had never mentioned educating Lexie about her heritage. He was Comanche, and Elaina was French and English, with a splash of Gypsy blood. The world was a melting pot of race, religion and color, he used to say. So why make an issue out of your child's ethnicity?

"When did he ask you to do that?" she asked.

"On the night he died," Nick answered, meeting her gaze with a haunted yet tender look.

The following morning Elaina and Lexie gathered in Nick's workshop for a leather-craft lesson. Nick taught classes at the youth center, something that surprised

Elaina. She hadn't known he had experience as a teacher.

Elaina glanced around, assessing the man and his workspace. His bench was a little messy, but his tools lined a backboard, each one easily accessible. Knives were protected in sheaths, and awls and punches rested in leather loops.

The air smelled of beeswax and mink oil. A cutting table and two sewing machines dominated a large portion of the room, shelves and benches occupying the rest. Leather ranged from vegetable-tanned hides to soft, furry skins. Trays of beads, hair-bone pipe and feathers reflected Nick's roots—a Comanche skilled in the art of cowboy crafts.

Elaina and Lexie sat at separate benches. While Lexie worked, Elaina marveled at her daughter's Christmas project. She was decorating holiday stockings Nick had designed. The pieces weren't sewn, but the patterns were cut, awaiting Lexie's imagination.

Elaina's and Nick's stockings were made from tooling leather, each in the shape of a cowboy boot, one smaller and slightly feminine, and the other bolder, with strong, masculine lines. Lexie's stocking was constructed similar to a knee-high moccasin, fringed at the edges and tall enough for an abundance of elf-inspired goodies.

The girl lifted the front piece of the larger cowboy boot. "Should I stamp your name on it, Uncle Nick?"

Gathering supplies for Elaina's project, he looked up. "Sure."

"Uncle? Nick? Or both?"

"How about *ahpi?* It means uncle in Comanche."

"Ahpi." Lexie tested the word the way he had pronounced it. "That's cool. How do you spell it?"

"A. P." He smiled at her. "That's easy. Not too many letters."

"Yes." She was still holding the boot, watching him with awe. "Can I call you that?"

"Of course you can." He stood near his workstation, his expression mirroring hers.

Elaina sat quietly. This was only their third day in Oklahoma, yet Lexie's relationship with Nick was blossoming already.

"Ap means father, too," he said.

"Really?" Intrigued, Lexie scooted to the end of her chair. "So a Comanche kid called their dad and their uncles *ap?"*

Nick nodded. "Let me see if I can explain why." He glanced at Elaina, then back at his niece. "It had to do with a marriage exchange. In the old days, brothers were potential mates to each other's wives."

"I don't understand." Lexie turned to Elaina. "Do you, Mom?"

"I'm not sure." She had an idea what potential mate meant, but she didn't want to say it out loud, not with her husband's twin just a few feet away.

Nick settled onto a chair, and Elaina's skin warmed.

His legs were spread, his hands resting on his thighs. Typical male posture, she thought nervously, as a silver buckle glinted at his waist. He was going to detail the marriage exchange, something Elaina wasn't sure she wanted to hear.

"In the old days, brothers lent each other their wives," Nick said. "The gesture was considered a gift from one to the other. But there wasn't supposed to be any jealousy between them. And the wife couldn't go to the other man on her own. Her loyalty remained with her husband."

Lexie made a face. "That's weird. I'd be mad at my husband if he did that. Especially if he had like ten brothers or something."

Nick chuckled, and Elaina sat like a pillar of salt, her heart banging against her breast. If she had been Grant's wife in an earlier century, would he have lent her to his twin? Would she have become Nick's gift? His occasional lover?

"I doubt they were that free with this exchange," he said to Lexie, addressing her comment. "And sure, it sounds strange, but it wasn't meant to dishonor the woman. One of the brothers might become her husband someday."

"How?" the young girl asked.

"If her husband died, a brother would take his place. He would protect her and the children."

Children who might have been his, Elaina noted. The wife could have borne the brother's babies as easily as those of her husband.

Nick left his chair and brought a box of supplies to Elaina, placing it on her bench. He was standing too close, she thought. She could smell his cologne—a deep, rich spice. Now the image wouldn't go away, the forbidden curiosity about making love with her husband's brother, of being given to him as a gift.

Nick bumped her arm as he leaned over, and she kept her eyes on her lap, on the wedding ring that shone on her finger. Shame coiled its way into her belly. How could she even think such immoral thoughts?

"In a sense, the Comanche used to form a marriage group," he said, still talking to Lexie about their ancestors. "Sisters were often married to the same man. It wasn't uncommon for a warrior to have more than one wife. So a child's mother and her sisters were all called *pia*. There's no separate word for aunt in the Comanche dialect. At least, not within a marriage group."

"Just like there's no separate word for uncle." Lexie searched through the alphabet stamps, setting aside an *A* and a *P*. She dampened the leather with a sponge, then picked up her mallet. "And that's why Daddy asked you to teach me about my heritage. Because you're my other *ap*."

Ap, Elaina thought. Her daughter was accepting Nick as a second father, but Lexie craved a paternal bond. She still cried for her daddy, still fell asleep with tears in her eyes.

Emotion swirled around the room, the only sound the

gentle tap of Lexie's hammer. Elaina glanced at Nick and saw that he watched her.

"We should get some work done, too," he said.

Unable to draw herself from his gaze, she studied him. Brothers lent each other their wives; they became fathers to each other's children. But that was in another century, she told herself as he brushed a lock of hair from his forehead.

His eyes had gone from brown to black, the pupils catching a glimmer of light. Elaina took an unsteady breath. He looked dark and erotic, a man who would kiss a woman in soft, secret places.

Why are you doing this to me? she wanted to ask. Why are you slipping into my subconscious? You're my brother-in-law, and I shouldn't be attracted to you.

"Elaina?"

"Yes?"

"Are you up for this?"

No, she thought, staring at the scatter of leather stars on her bench.

"Yes, of course," she responded. Her involvement in this project was important to Lexie. It was Christmas-time, and the stars were for the tree Nick had promised Lexie they would buy tomorrow. "Just tell me what to do."

As he moved closer, his shoulder brushed hers. "There are a lot of different ways to decorate them."

He reached into the box and withdrew samples of completed ornaments. Some were stamped with traditional Western patterns, and others displayed vibrant Native American designs, the points trimmed in suede lace. No two were alike. Instead, each creation reflected the level and skill of the artist. She didn't have to ask if his students had made them.

Reaching for one that caught her eye, she held it up to the light. An intricate beaded design covered the entire star, shimmering as if it had just fallen from the sky.

"This is beautiful," she said, looking from the ornament to Nick.

He looked back at her, and an unwelcome, unnamed heat filled her veins. He was beautiful, too. But unlike the glittering star, her brother-in-law was dark and dangerously forbidden.

Later that night, Nick couldn't sleep. He got out of bed, slipped on a pair of jeans and boots, then shoved his arms into a jacket. Nothing calmed a restless night like the outdoors. Humidity, rain, snow, brisk winds. Nick didn't care. No matter what mood Mother Earth was in, she managed to soothe him.

He made it as far as the living room before he saw Elaina. She sat on a sturdy recliner, her feet tucked beneath her. The television flickered with black-and-white images, the volume barely audible.

Her hair cascaded in loose waves, and she wore silky white pajamas. In profile, her features were classically feminine, with a sweep of dark lashes and a slim nose.

Her lips were neither strained nor relaxed. She stared at the TV in an almost trancelike state.

"Elaina?" He said her name, knowing he couldn't slip out the front door unnoticed.

She turned, and then blinked when she saw him. "Nick."

They gazed at each other for a moment, and he realized how often they got caught in one of those quiet, awkward stares.

"Is something wrong?" she asked.

"No." He shifted his stance. She looked ghostlike in the flickering light, her pajamas shimmering against creamy skin.

"The horses aren't sick?"

"No." He glanced at the scuffed, turned-up tips of his boots. He was dressed to go out, yet he hadn't told her why. But running into Elaina at this hour stunned his senses, dulling his brain. She wasn't wearing a bra, and he could see the faint outline of her nipples. He hadn't meant to look, but his eyes had strayed in that direction. And now he was examining his feet like a tongue-tied teenager.

"I'm having trouble falling asleep," he said finally, lifting his gaze. "So I'm going to sit on the porch awhile."

"Can I join you?" She pushed a wave of hair off her shoulder. "I can't sleep, either."

He wanted to say no, that he preferred to be alone. She was an elegant, silk-clad distraction. He was

sexually attracted to his brother's wife, and that made
him uncomfortable, even though he had vowed to marry
her.

"It's been cold at night," he warned. "And windy."

"I don't mind. I brought a winter coat."

"All right." Why argue the point? She must need a
gust of fresh air, too.

He leaned against the wall while she darted into her
room. When she returned, her silky pajamas were
covered with a big, bulky sheepskin coat. Nick couldn't
hide an amused smile.

"You expecting a blizzard?"

"You said it was cold."

"Yeah, I guess I did."

Once outside, they sat in weathered pine chairs, the
sky a vast shade of midnight. A maze of trees land-
scaped the yard. Some were shedding leaves and others
were bare, tall and gray in the moonlight. The porch
light cast a shallow glow, and Nick turned to look at
Elaina.

Her collar was turned up, and her hands were tucked
snugly in her pockets. The wind blew with a furious
howl, tousling her copper-tinted hair.

Nick inhaled the chilly December air, and to keep
himself from staring at Elaina, he focused on the sky.
"There's a few stars out."

"Yes, just a scatter." She angled her chair toward his
with the scrape of wood against wood. "Do you do this
often?"

He shrugged. "Often enough, I suppose. Sometimes my mind just won't shut down, and that makes sleeping impossible."

"I know the feeling."

Her face was a blend of shadow and light, her voice quiet. She removed her hands from her pockets, and he glanced down and saw the diamond on her finger. Was he supposed to buy her a new ring or suggest she continue to wear the one Grant had given her? There were no rules to follow. Nothing he could count on to make this situation easier.

But Nick realized he had to do it tonight. He had to ask Elaina to marry him. Two years had passed, more than enough time for him to fulfill his vow.

They gazed at each other in the silence, and the moment turned soft and quiet. Moonlight shone in her eyes, tiny flecks of gold in all that impossible blue. He imagined touching her cheek, her hair, the delicate column of her neck.

Nick frowned. If he lost himself in lust, in the heat she made him feel, this proposal would be even more difficult.

"Elaina, there's something important I need to discuss with you."

She watched him, waiting for him to continue.

He did, after another second of nervous silence. "You know that my brother asked me to take care of Lexie, to teach her about being Comanche. But before he died, he talked to me about you, too."

The light in her eyes flickered, and Nick saw a flash of pain, a woman missing the man she had loved. "What did he say?"

"Grant wanted me to protect you." Pausing to breathe, he let the words settle. "The way a Comanche brother would have done in another century."

Her voice quavered. "I don't understand."

Yes, you do, he thought. Deep down you do. You know what a Comanche marriage exchange means.

Nick glanced at the sky, at the scatter of stars. "When Grant was dying in my arms, I vowed to take his place, to become your husband and Lexie's father." Shifting his gaze, he looked directly into her eyes, felt his own sting with the memory. "I'm proposing, Elaina. In the name of my brother, I'm asking you to marry me."

Four

Elaina couldn't breathe, couldn't get air into her lungs, couldn't still her runaway heart. "I…" She twisted her wedding ring, felt her fingers tremble. "Are you sure that's what Grant meant? I can't believe he would…" Expect me to marry his brother, she thought, live with a man I barely know.

"He was dying, but he knew what he was saying." Nick leaned forward. "I vowed to follow the old way, and that means you're my potential mate. You were my brother's wife, and now he's gone. It's my responsibility to take his place."

"This doesn't make sense," she said, fighting the confusion. "I thought Grant loved me."

"He did. And that's exactly why he couldn't bear for

you to be alone. He needed to know that there would be someone in your life after he was gone. Someone he trusted."

Battling the heaviness in her chest, Elaina couldn't grasp a response. She couldn't think clearly.

As she twisted her ring again, Nick continued. "Our union won't be based on love. I don't expect you to love me. That's not what this is about."

"It's based on an ancient tradition that doesn't fit into a modern world," she countered, struggling with the idea that her husband had given her to his twin. "Marriage is sacred."

"And so is this vow. I promise to treat you with kindness and respect. And that's all I expect in return. That's all Grant was asking of us."

She moistened her lips, wishing she had a glass of water. Suddenly her mouth had gone dry.

"I can't force you to marry me, but I implore you to consider it," he said.

She tried to picture herself living with him, sharing a closet, a bathroom, a bed. What about sex? she wondered nervously. Was that part of the kindness and respect he was offering?

She couldn't possibly sleep with Nick, could she? They were practically strangers, in-laws battling an awkward attraction.

"Elaina?"

"Yes?" She glanced up and saw him studying her through those dark, hypnotic eyes.

"If you think you're going to meet someone else someday. If you think there will be someone who makes you feel the way Grant did, then I'll understand if you say no." He shifted his chair, scraping it against the wood porch. "But that won't stop me from keeping a close eye on you and Lexie. Or from being her father. In my soul, both of you will still be mine."

Because he had made a vow to Grant, she thought. To his dying brother. To her husband.

"There will never be anyone else," she said, thinking about Grant. Elaina would never fall in love again. Once in a lifetime was enough. Losing Grant had taught her that love, the kind that pierced your soul and constricted your heart, wasn't worth the risk.

She continued to hold Nick's gaze. "What about you?" she asked, feeling her breath hitch.

He frowned in confusion. "What do you mean?"

"What if you're destined to meet someone special someday?"

He shook his head, hair falling across his forehead. "I'm not that kind of guy."

Of course not, she thought. He'd made a commitment to his brother, but he couldn't give his heart to a woman. Nick Bluestone accepted that side of himself.

"Will you think about my proposal, Elaina? Will you consider what Grant wanted?"

Dear God. She had to, she realized. She couldn't discard her husband's last request, the words he'd spoken as he lay bleeding. Grant had died in Nick's arms, but his last thoughts had been of her and Lexie.

"I can't make a decision overnight," she said, tears welling in her eyes. "I need some time."

"Are you going talk to Lexie about it?"

Elaina nodded. "Yes, but not right away. I have to sort this out for myself first." She needed to grasp the reality of what was actually happening. This seemed like a dream, a whirlwind of emotions she couldn't control. The world had zapped her back in time, pulling her into the center of an ancient Comanche custom.

A marriage exchange, she thought. Wild, dark-eyed Nick had vowed to marry his brother's widow. Somehow that didn't seem possible, yet it had happened.

"I won't push you," he said, meeting her gaze. "I'll wait for your decision. I'll wait until you're ready."

"Thank you," she whispered, not knowing what else to say.

Daylight shimmered, but Elaina was still thinking about the night before. Nick Bluestone had asked her to marry him. Her brother-in-law, Grant's twin. None of this seemed real.

"What do you think of Lawton, Mom?"

She nearly jumped at the sound of her daughter's voice. On this breezy afternoon, Elaina sat on the passenger's side of Nick's truck, and Lexie rode in the crew cab.

"It's pretty," she managed, glancing out the window.

Lawton was the third largest city in Oklahoma, yet it seemed to offer the advantages that came with small-town living. The crime rate was low, and beyond the city limits, farmers, cattlemen and cowboys ruled the historic plains.

Land was plentiful, with a variety of country homes and ranches dotting the landscape. Elaina imagined the area was breathtaking in the spring, when greenery flourished and flowers bloomed.

"There's a wildlife refuge in the Wichita Mountains," Nick said.

Lexie leaned forward. "Really? What kinds of animals are there?"

He caught his niece's gaze in the rearview mirror. "Buffalo, elk, deer, some longhorn cattle. But I think there's a livestock show going on this weekend. We can visit the refuge another time, when it's not so busy."

While they headed to the Christmas tree lot, Lexie and Nick discussed their agenda, with Nick suggesting points of interest. He offered to take them to the Fort Sill Museum on Monday and to the Museum of the Great Plains on Tuesday. Next Friday they could catch a play at the community theater, and on Saturday night he wanted them to see the Boulevard of Lights.

"Wow." Lexie's eyes lit up. "We've got lots of stuff to do."

Yes, Elaina thought, he wanted them to enjoy

Lawton, the place he expected them to live. Marrying Nick would mean moving to Oklahoma.

"Will you take me into town later?" she asked. "I think I should rent a car."

He turned onto another country road. "What for?"

"So Lexie and I can get around by ourselves when you're working." And so Elaina could go to market and the mall without having to rely on Nick. She needed a chance to get away, to think about his proposal without having him nearby. He was too much of a distraction— a handsome, confusing distraction.

"That's fine, but don't waste money on a rental. You can borrow my truck whenever you need it."

Elaina looked around the cab. Yeah, right. This big, beefy, four-wheel drive? The one with the floor shift? "Thanks, but I'd rather rent a sedan or something."

He sent her a sideways glance, the glare of an offended man. "Is there something wrong with my truck?"

"It's a stick shift."

"So?"

"So I don't know how to drive a stick."

The glare turned to shock. "You're kidding?"

"I never had cause to learn. I started with an automatic, so I stayed with an automatic." And the sports cars Grant used to favor didn't interest her. She preferred simple, easy-to-control compacts. Not aerodynamic bullets that sped into traffic. Or trucks, she thought, that could mow a house down.

Nick pulled off to the side of the road and killed the engine, and Elaina knew exactly what he had in mind.

"No way," she said.

"What's going on?" Lexie unbuckled her seat belt and poked her head over Nick's shoulder.

"I'm going to teach your mom how to drive a stick."

Elaina glanced at her daughter. "No, he's not." With a pointed look at Nick, she crossed her arms. "And don't you dare make an issue out of this."

"Sure, fine." He flashed a boyish grin. "I'll bet you drive as bad as you dance, anyway."

"Oh, good grief." She punched his arm, and they both laughed. During the traditional money dance at her wedding, Nick had paid a generous sum to dance with her. The best man and the bride. The song had been a dreamy California ballad, only they hadn't made a very graceful pair. "As I recall, that was your fault."

"Mine? You were the one who kept tripping."

"And you were the one who kept stepping on my dress."

They smiled at each other, knowing full well whose fault it had been. Grant had been making faces at them, grinning and mugging from the sidelines. He'd made dancing impossible. And fun. Elaina and Nick had laughed through the entire song.

"It was one of those beach tunes," he said, as if he'd just read her mind. "About some young guy who falls in love with this little surfer girl."

"I remember." The lyrics were sweet and simple, she thought. The melody as natural as an ocean breeze. "The DJ kept playing all those old songs."

"Yeah." He ran a hand through his hair. "Do you know what I was thinking when we were out there, stumbling all over each other?"

She looked into his eyes and caught the corner of his smile. That boyish, more-crooked-than-Grant's smile. "No. What?"

"That you were the perfect bride."

Her heart went soft. "It was the happiest day of my life."

"I know. It showed."

And now their gazes were locked, the memory soft and stirring. The past and the present were blending. A mixture of beauty and warmth.

Elaina moistened her lips. He'd called her the perfect bride, this man who'd vowed to marry her. She couldn't help but wonder how it would feel to kiss him, if he tasted as potent as he looked.

"How come we're just sitting here?" Lexie asked impatiently.

Elaina's heart slammed against her breast, and Nick broke eye contact instantly.

"Because your uncle is going to teach me to drive his truck." It was the only thing she could think of to say, the only excuse she could give for staring at Nick, for allowing him to stare back at her. "Aren't you, Nick?"

"Yeah, but we have to switch seats." He glanced back

at Lexie, his voice huskier than it should have been. "Buckle up, kiddo. Your mom's taking the wheel."

Elaina exited the car, and as Nick passed her on his way to the passenger's side, she inhaled a gust of the wind-ravaged air.

Repositioning herself, she adjusted the seat, then fiddled with the mirrors. "Give me a minute," she said, doing her damnedest not to look too closely at Nick. A piece of his hair had fallen over his forehead, giving him a rebellious edge. But then, that was part of Nick's appeal. The rugged Comanche in frayed jeans and scuffed leather boots.

His truck, with its wide tires and polished chrome, fit him to a tee. The silver bands that shackled his wrists glinted against sun-burnished skin, and under his shirt a tribal tattoo decorated his navel.

She hadn't seen it up close, but she'd caught a glimpse of it when he'd gone swimming with Grant. And yes, it was kind of sexy. Something wild and primitive for his lovers to kiss.

"Elaina?"

"What?" With a slight jerk, she turned to see him watching her.

"Are you ready?"

"Yes. Yes. Of course," she said, knowing full well she wasn't anywhere near being ready. Not with an image of his bare stomach clouding her mind.

"I'm going to teach you how to shift," he said. "But

don't start the truck. Not yet. Just set the emergency brake so we can do a dry run."

She pushed the lever. "Got it."

"Good." He leaned in close, and Elaina's pulse ignited. She could smell the spice of his aftershave, the clean, brisk scent.

She glanced at his jaw. And then at his mouth. His lips were slightly chapped, she noticed. But he spent a lot of time outdoors. Of course, that's what gave his skin that rough, wind-burned quality. That sexy, Indian-cowboy look.

Elaina's heart bumped her breast. He'd actually proposed. Her wild, bachelor brother-in-law.

"The shift pattern is like the letter *H*," he explained.

She did her damnedest to listen, to comprehend each gear and when to use them. But her wandering gaze drifted back to his mouth. He moistened his lips, wetting them with his tongue. Instinctively, she wet hers, too.

"It's time to practice," he said.

She blew a quick breath. "Should I start the engine now?"

"No. You're just going to go through the motions." He bent his head, checking the position of her feet. "Push in the clutch," he instructed. "Good. Now you're ready to shift."

Elaina grabbed hold of the knob, but when Nick covered her hand with his, a jolt of electricity shot from her fingers to her toes. "What are you doing?"

"Helping. We'll do this together until you're used to it."

She tried to act casual, to pretend his touch hadn't sent her into a state of feminine shock. His palms were slightly callused, and hers were clammy with sweat.

While they practiced the H pattern, Lexie complained from the back seat. "This is boring."

Nick glanced over his shoulder. "Give your mom a chance. She's almost ready."

"Almost ready" meant applying all that she'd learned.

With her foot on the clutch, she started the engine. Next she shifted into first gear, and then slowly let out the clutch. As soon as she felt it take hold, she gave the truck some gas and released the emergency brake.

It seemed like a lot of unnecessary work to get a vehicle moving.

But move it did, and in no time Elaina was cruising down an isolated country road and shifting successfully into Second.

She turned to give her daughter a smug look. "Are you bored now?"

"No, but there's a stop sign up ahead, Mom. So you should probably pay attention to what you're doing."

She focused on the road. "I see it."

"Don't forget to downshift," Lexie prodded.

"Yes, Little-miss-know-it-all. When's the last time you drove a car?"

Nick didn't say a word, so Elaina proceeded to stop,

hitting her mark perfectly. "See?" Proud as a flamboyant peacock, she lifted her nose in the air.

As she sat, mentally congratulating herself, her foot slipped off the clutch. The truck lurched forward and stalled.

Nick and Lexie burst out laughing.

Stunned and a little peeved, Elaina glared at both of them. "My foot slipped."

"Sure it did." Nick bit down on his bottom lip, clearly fighting the urge to laugh again.

Determined to prove her point, Elaina restarted the engine and got the truck moving. But her determination was short-lived.

The vehicle hiccuped down the road, stalling every time she let out the clutch and gave the truck either too much or not enough gas. Her rhythm, damn it, was shot.

"You're not helping," she snapped at Nick. He was too busy hooting up a storm with Lexie to give Elaina proper instructions.

By the time they reached the Christmas tree lot, Nick's eyes were watering and Lexie's sides ached.

Serves them right, Elaina thought.

The Christmas tree lot sat on a small hill, but she wasn't about to ask Nick how to tackle it. She would figure this one out on her own.

Her attempt went from frustration to humiliation. She couldn't get the truck over the hump in the driveway. Once again, it stalled.

The man behind her whaled on his horn.

And kept whaling as Elaina struggled to get the truck going.

Nick and Lexie were beside themselves, laughing their fool heads off. She wanted to throttle both of them. Everyone at the lot was watching.

"Come on, lady, move it!"

"Merry Christmas to you, too," she muttered. "You old grump."

"Should I flip him the bird?" Lexie asked in a young, sweet voice, making Nick roar even harder.

Mortified, she spun around to glare at her daughter. "Don't you dare." The last thing she needed was her twelve-year-old making obscene gestures from the back seat. "And you." She jabbed Nick's chest. "Stop encouraging Lexie to be a delinquent and do something to get this truck moving."

"Yes, ma'am." He offered to take the wheel, and, while they switched places, the man behind them blasted his horn again.

"Don't do anything macho," Elaina warned.

"I won't," Nick promised. But as he started the truck, he sent Lexie a playful wink, then pulled into the parking lot with a noisy screech, stirring a cloud of dust in their wake.

Elaina and Lexie sipped hot chocolate while Nick examined the Christmas tree. He'd placed it in front of a window in the living room, a six-foot blue spruce with silvery branches. Elaina thought it was lovely—fragrant and nicely shaped.

Tilting his head to one side, Nick frowned. "Is it just me, or does it look a little lopsided?"

"I'm not sure." Lexie placed her cup on an end table, and then gave the tree a serious study. "It could be a tad crooked."

"Yeah." A smile ghosted around his mouth. "Of course, we're both still dizzy from your mom's driving, so we can't be sure."

Lexie grinned at her uncle. "No kidding. I wasn't sure if we'd survive all that bumper-car action."

"At least she didn't grind the gears," he said.

"She didn't? Are you sure? We were probably laughing too hard to hear it."

Elaina rolled her eyes. "Very funny."

They were certainly enjoying this silly little game, she thought. Of course, now that the humiliation was over, she was secretly pleased that Lexie had learned to belly laugh again. Nick seemed to be a positive influence on her daughter. The Comanche bad boy and the juvenile delinquent. They made quite a pair.

She gave them her toughest-mom look. "The tree is just fine, Heckle and Jeckle. So you two can stop grinning and find something else to do."

"No problem." Nick's lips were still twitching, even as he put on an air of seriousness. "I'll get the Christmas lights and see if they still work. I think they're in the basement. Then again, I might have stored them in the garage."

Elaina shook her head, realizing how disorderly he was. So unlike Grant, who used to color code his clothes, arranging them carefully in a walk-in closet. Nick's denim-and-cotton wardrobe was probably hanging haphazardly, tilting like his crescent smile.

Lexie plopped onto the couch and reached for the remote. "Will you fix an early dinner, Mom? I'm getting hungry."

"Sure." Elaina headed into the kitchen, then looked through the fridge and decided on meat loaf. The ingredients were readily available, although she doubted that had been deliberate on Nick's part.

In no time, she became absorbed in her task. She made bread crumbs and diced onions. She enjoyed keeping busy, and the kitchen was cozy, even if the curtains were much too plain and the counter space a bit too stingy.

Shaping the meat loaf, she looked up when Lexie came into the room.

"Mom. There's some weird girl who keeps skating in front of the house. I think she's spying on us."

Stunned, Elaina stared at her daughter. Paranoia hadn't been part of Lexie's depression, but anything was possible. One day of laughter didn't mean lifelong happiness. "Skating?"

"Yeah, you know. In-line skates."

"She's allowed to use the street, honey." Although a

bumpy road didn't seem like the safest place to skate. "There are no sidewalks around here."

"I know, but she keeps going back and forth and looking at the house."

The meat loaf went into the oven, and Elaina turned to wash her hands. "Maybe you're overreacting a little. I honestly doubt she's spying on us."

"I knew you wouldn't believe me." Lexie stormed out of the kitchen, her tiny body weighted down with baggy clothes. She looked frail yet tough. The blue jeans that rode her hips were fraying at the hem, and her heavy black shoes made a hard, defiant thud.

The sound echoed in Elaina's ears. Unsure of what to do, she stood like a statue, aching for her only child. The quick bursts of anger had become commonplace, but she would never get used to them.

Soon, she thought, Lexie would be slamming doors. Or staring into space like a zombie, refusing to speak. And in no time, tears would flow—hers and Lexie's.

Releasing a shaky breath, Elaina squared her shoulders. The least she could do was confront her daughter's paranoia, even if it meant peering out the window at some poor unsuspecting neighbor.

Elaina entered the living room. Lexie sat on the sofa, flipping channels with the remote. The screen blinked on and off in a disturbing vignette of color and sound.

"Is she still out there?" Elaina asked.

Lexie shrugged. "What do you care?"

"I'm curious." And worried, she thought. So worried

about my daughter. "Maybe I should check." Kneeling on the couch, she moved the curtain aside.

The girl in question was rolling down the street, her skates jittery on the rough country road. She wore Western-cut jeans and a blue windbreaker, long, dark hair blowing behind her.

She didn't look like a stalker or an international spy. She looked, Elaina thought, like a kid out to enjoy what was left of the day. A normal, healthy, happy kid.

Elaina watched as the youth made a U-turn, heading in their direction. But as she neared the driveway, she turned and craned her head as far as it would go. Like a turtle emerging from its shell, Elaina noted. The girl was a tad curious.

"I'll bet she saw you, Lexie."

"Yeah, right. And now she wants to be instant friends."

"She looks about your age." Taller, but just as lean, with a body that had yet to develop. "Why don't you go outside and say hello?"

"Get real, Mom. That's so dorky."

And moping around the house was cool? "It was just a suggestion."

Elaina turned away, but as she did, she caught sight of the skater speeding by again. Only this time, when the girl glanced toward the house, she stumbled and landed headfirst in the road, her hands skidding across the pavement.

"Oh, my goodness."

Reacting like the teacher she was, Elaina bolted out the front door, armed with years of experience. Playground accidents didn't panic her anymore, but she knew even the smallest tumble could result in a twisted ankle or a bloody nose.

"Are you all right?"

The young girl was already peeling herself off the pavement, a stunned and embarrassed look on her face. She had a golden complexion, slightly flushed, with deep-set eyes, a full mouth and broad cheekbones. Part Indian, Elaina thought, just like Lexie.

"I fell."

"I know. I saw. Do you need some help?"

The child shrugged, and then frowned at her hands. They were scraped, blackened from the road and oozing blood.

Elaina moved closer. "Come inside, and I'll get you cleaned up."

"Is Nick home?"

"Yes, but he's in the basement."

"Is Ryan here?"

"No." She had no idea who he was, but this didn't seem like the time to ask. The girl's injured hands must be burning. "It's just my daughter and me. And Nick, of course. I'll help you get your skates off."

When they entered the house, Lexie was lurking near the door. They went into the kitchen, where the meat loaf had begun to cook, filling the room with a pleasant aroma.

After Elaina cleaned and assessed the wounds, which turned out to be more dirt than blood, she introduced Lexie, who stood back uncomfortably, shy and uncertain about their visitor.

"I'm Starr," the other girl said. "My parents were on some we-want-our-daughter-to-shine kick when they named me. They're divorced now. I live down the street with my mom." She met Lexie's wary gaze, her head tilting curiously. "You're staying here for Christmas?"

"Yes."

"And Nick's your uncle?"

"Yes."

"That's cool. My mom and I live with my grandparents." Her smile was quick and friendly. "What do you think of Ryan?"

Lexie squinted. "Who?"

"The boy who works for your uncle. Ryan helps Nick with his leather stuff."

An alarm went off in Elaina's head. Apparently Starr had been spying on the house. Hoping, it appeared, to see the elusive Ryan.

The girl nearly sighed. "He rides a motorcycle, but he always parks it in back, so I never know when he's here. You're so lucky. You'll get to see him all the time."

Now Lexie seemed intrigued. But motorcycles fascinated her, Elaina thought.

Lexie inched closer to Starr. "How old is he?"

"Sixteen."

"Is his bike a Harley?"

The other girl shrugged. "I think so. It's kind of big and noisy."

"My uncle is teaching me to how to do leather work," Lexie offered, trying to sound more grown-up. "So I guess that means I'll probably have to hang out with Ryan."

Starr's eyes all but glittered. "Do you think I could learn, too?"

Lexie smiled, clearly enjoying her newfound power. "Maybe."

Starr shot Elaina a quick glance, and then turned back to Lexie. "Do you want to go outside?"

When her daughter accepted the other girl's invitation, Elaina leaned against the counter, realizing she was being shut out of the conversation. But then, heart-throbs were rarely discussed in front of someone's mother. And now that Ryan was in the picture, Lexie didn't seem to think Starr was weird or that going outside to make friends with her was dorky.

The girls shuffled out the door, and Elaina breathed a sigh of relief. Starr seemed like quite a character, a bit boy crazy, but her preteen crush on Ryan appeared normal enough. And by the time Starr was through singing Ryan's praises, Lexie would probably have a crush on him, too.

And here I am, she thought. A thirty-five-year-old with a crush of my own. But then, Nick, with his thread-bare jeans, sterling wristbands and tribal tattoo, would make any woman take notice.

Of course, he hadn't asked just any woman to marry him. He'd asked her. His brother's widow.

"What am I going to do?" she whispered to herself.

Call Jackie, her mind answered. Get some advice from a friend. Spill your soul. Let it off your chest.

Jackie Monroe answered the phone in a vibrant voice. She was an L.A. dynamo who owned a fashionable boutique on upper Sunset. She was also Elaina's very single, very feminist neighbor at the condominium complex.

"What's up?" Jackie asked.

Elaina leaned against the counter. She'd closed the kitchen door, but she still hoped Nick didn't come barreling in and catch her on the phone. Suddenly she felt like a teenager whispering about the hottest boy at school.

After she went into vivid detail about the marriage proposal, Jackie blew a sultry whistle. "That hunky brother of Grant's is offering to be your knight-in-denim-armor?"

"Jackie, this is serious." She paused to glance at the door. "And when did you see Nick?"

"Grant introduced me to him once. They were on their way to the pool. Great body, long hair, tattoo on his navel."

Elaina made a face at the phone. Apparently her girlfriend had taken an up-close-and-personal inventory of Nick Bluestone. "His hair isn't long anymore."

"Too bad," the other woman commented.

She let the remark pass. Jackie had been out of the country the summer Grant had been killed, the summer Nick had cut his hair. "I have no idea what to do."

"Sleep with him," came the blunt reply.

Elaina nearly laughed. Trust Jackie to cut to the quick. The free-spirited blonde had a lover for every season. She pictured Jackie sitting in her art deco living room, dressed in a Moroccan caftan, her acrylic nails painted a fire-engine shade of red.

She glanced at her own proper attire, her own subtle, blush-pink manicure. If only she could be that daring. "I'm supposed to marry him for sex?"

"I didn't say marry him, I said sleep with him. Get the man out of your system."

"You know I can't do that. I'm not the affair type."

"Then answer this. Are you seriously considering his proposal?"

"Yes." Elaina nodded firmly. "But I'm not sure why."

"Because," the other woman said softly, "deep down you respect Nick for what he did. I mean, here's a modern man who made an old-world promise to his dying brother. And that promise involved you and Lexie. That's some pretty heavy stuff."

Jackie was right. Elaina couldn't cast aside the heartfelt pledge Nick had made to Grant. What he'd agreed to do was tragically romantic. And the woman in her, the young widow who slept alone each night in a big, lonely bed, missed the comfort of a husband's strong, safe arms.

So in a sense, Nick Bluestone was offering to be her knight-in-denim-armor. And that was something she just couldn't ignore.

Five

Nick glanced at Elaina. She sat beside him in the truck, looking like what she was—a woman capable of making a man's blood swim. Her chestnut hair, twisted into a loose topknot, shimmered with strands of copper, and her hands were clasped delicately on her lap. He suspected she was nervous.

"My friends are anxious to meet you," he said.

"Did you tell them Lexie wasn't coming?"

He nodded. His niece had decided to spend the day with Starr instead. He envisioned them munching on potato chips and chatting about the latest boy band to hit the teen idol scene. With a twelve-year-old neighbor to keep her busy, Lexie seemed to be snapping out of her melancholy right quick.

"Do your friends know about you and me?" Elaina paused to take a breath. "About the proposal?"

"Yes." He'd had to tell someone. "I grew up with Tony Horn. Grant and I hung around with him when we were kids. And Vera, his grandmother, treats me like one of her own."

He turned onto a tree-lined street. He supposed he should warn Elaina about the older woman. Tony's grandmother might seem like a bit of a matchmaker.

"Vera's been trying to marry me off for ages. She's pretty excited about this proposal." He shrugged, hoping to ease Elaina's mind. "So if she starts telling you what a good boy I am, just take it in stride."

Elaina shifted in her seat. He felt her gaze slide over him. He cursed himself for getting warm, for wanting Grant's woman so badly.

"You're hardly a boy, Nick."

"I am to Vera," he responded, pushing the pent-up air from his lungs.

"Was she fond of Grant, too?"

"Yeah. She was crazy about him." And disappointed, Nick thought, that Grant had never brought his wife and child to Oklahoma.

He steered the truck down a gravel driveway and parked in front of a modest house. Lace curtains trimmed the living-room windows, and leafy plants flourished in an attractive flower bed, giving the home a feminine appeal.

For a moment Nick stared at the yard. He and Grant had played here as children. They'd climbed the trees with Tony, pretending to swing like Tarzan, pounding their chests and yelling at the top of their lungs.

"This is Vera's place," he said, shaking off the memory. "Tony lives about a mile away." But Tony would be at his grandmother's this afternoon, curious to meet Elaina.

Nick ushered Elaina up the front steps, but before he could ring the bell, the door flew open. Tony appeared on the other side, an unlit cigarette dangling from the corner of his lips. Tall and lanky, with a mischievous sense of humor, Tony used to get himself in trouble as a kid, firing spit wads and making faces behind teachers' backs, Nick remembered.

"Hey, Nicky," he said, grinning. "And you must be Elaina. Wow. You look just like your picture."

She blinked. "My picture?"

"From your wedding. You and Grant," he clarified.

"That was a long time ago. I'm sure I've changed." She smiled at Tony and smoothed her sweater in a self-conscious gesture. It clung to her curves in a lethal stretch of body-hugging knit. Nick couldn't help but follow the motion of her hands.

"Goodness, gracious, Tony, move out of the way and let them in." Vera bustled behind her grandson, fists on plump hips, dark eyes sparkling behind wire-rimmed glasses.

Instantly the older lady fawned over Elaina. "You're

beautiful," she said, then turned to Nick. "Oh, Nicky. She's beautiful."

He nodded and smiled at the gorgeous woman in question. She blushed, and he winked, feeling like a flirtatious teenager, a boy dying to get to first base.

Tony chuckled beside him, clearly reading Nick's embarrassing thoughts.

Within ten minutes Vera and Elaina were engaged in conversation. Tony's eleven-month-old son squirmed on Vera's lap, the apple of his great-grandma's eye. The kid had inherited Tony's cockeyed grin, as well as his dad's penchant for mischief.

Tony motioned to the door. "Let's get some air," he said to Nick.

The moment they were seated on the porch steps, Tony lit the cigarette. He had been smoking since their teenage years, a habit that had gotten him suspended from high school many times.

"So is she going to marry you?" he asked.

Nick shrugged. "I don't know. She hasn't made a decision yet."

Tony flicked his ashes a bit carelessly, dropping them onto his shoe. "There's still time to back out of this, you know."

"Why would I want to do that?"

"Because marriage is the commitment of a lifetime, buddy. The final plunge."

Nick gave his friend a level stare. "You did it," he said, thinking about Tony's patient wife, a woman who put up with her husband's sidetracked personality. Tony rarely finished anything he started. He'd mow half the lawn or paint half a fence, leaving his neighbors shaking their heads.

"True, I did. But I didn't agree to marry my brother's widow."

"Your brother is still alive. And I told you why I proposed to Elaina."

"I know. Because Grant asked you to." The cigarette bobbed. "But come on, Nicky. This whole thing is a little weird."

Nick tamed the hair falling onto his forehead, pushing it back with a rough motion. "I know what I'm doing. I've had two years to think about this." Two years of fear and guilt and tangled emotions. "I believe in the old way, and if Elaina says yes, then I'm going to marry her."

Both men fell silent. Tony blew smoke into the wind, and Nick gazed at the sky. Clouds moved across a misty stretch of blue, like weightless pillows floating across the heavens.

Elaina was his destiny, he thought, reaffirming his decision. The Comanche vow he couldn't deny. The woman he yearned to touch.

"I'll bet you've got the honeymoon all figured out."

Nick turned to look at his friend. Tony's mouth curved into a knowing grin.

He shrugged, making light of the other man's comment. He wanted to take Elaina to his cabin, to show her his mountaintop sanctuary, but he wasn't about to admit it.

Nick intended to keep those syrupy feelings to himself.

Less than a week later, Elaina sat on the edge of her daughter's bed. Lexie still sported the jeans and T-shirt she'd worn to dinner, but she'd flung her winter coat over a chair.

"Starr's grandma and grandpa are really nice," Lexie said. She sat cross-legged in the center of the bed, one side of her hair clipped with a rose-shaped barrette, the petals decorated with tiny jewels.

"Really?" Elaina tilted her head. Lexie hadn't worn a hair ornament since kindergarten, and even then she had stomped her feet and whined about ribbons, flowers and bows. "So you had a nice time with Starr's family?"

Lexie nodded. "We ate at a Mexican restaurant, and the tacos were really good. They have everything here, Mom. It's kind of like L.A., only better."

Better. That meant her daughter was settling in, feeling at home in Oklahoma. "I like your barrette."

"Oh." Lexie touched the rose. "Starr gave it to me. Lots of models wear them. We saw one almost just like it in a magazine."

Elaina smiled. This was a conversation she had never expected to have with her little tomboy. "You should give Starr something in return."

"I'm going to make her a fringed shoulder bag." She

shifted her position, adjusting her legs. "*Ap* says I'm really good at leather work. He's showing me how to do stuff from his advanced classes. Of course, he still has to help, but I'm getting it."

"Good. I'm glad." Elaina placed her hands on her lap, felt her heartbeat quicken. "Honey, there's something I need to talk to you about. Something that involves all of us—you, me and Nick." Clasping her fingers, she paused. "And Daddy, too."

Lexie's eyes grew wide. "What is it, Mom? What's wrong?"

"I didn't say there was anything wrong."

"But you sound worried."

Just confused, she thought. Struggling to make a decision. "Do you remember what your uncle told us about the Comanche? About how brothers used to look after each other's families? Especially if one of them died?"

The young girl nodded.

"Well, that's what Daddy asked Uncle Nick to do."

"I know. That's why *Ap* is teaching me about my heritage."

Elaina closed her eyes, opened them a second later. "That's true. But before Daddy died, he also asked your uncle to marry me. He wanted all of us to live together as a family."

"Oh, wow. You and Uncle Nick. Just like in the old days." Lexie came forward to sit beside her mother. "Do you want to marry him?"

She glanced at her wedding ring, at the marquee-cut diamond on her finger. "It's what your father wanted."

"But what about you, Mom?"

"I like your uncle." And she ached to touch him, kiss him, feel his naked body next to hers. Nick Bluestone had become her hot, sexy, guilt-ridden fantasy. "But I barely know him."

"He'd probably try to make you happy."

Kindness and respect. Elaina knew it had been a genuine offer. "Yes, he's a good man." She reached for her daughter's hand. "How does this make you feel, Lexie? I really need to know."

The child's eyes filled with tears. "It makes me miss Daddy, but it makes me feel closer to him, too. He was thinking about us before he died. And he wanted to be sure we wouldn't be all alone." Sniffing, she rubbed her nose. "It kind of makes sense. Brothers looking after each other's families. Uncle Nick, *Ap,* he'll protect us."

Lexie is accepting this, Elaina realized. She needed the security Grant had arranged for her. And she longed to stay in Oklahoma where she felt secure, where her uncle, her second father, could tuck her in at night.

"Are you going to marry him, Mom?"

Am I? she wondered. "I don't know. Maybe. Probably. I'll sleep on it, then make a decision tomorrow." After all, she couldn't drag this on forever. Each day that passed made her more anxious.

"Okay." Lexie leaned into her, and they hugged.

And when she stroked her daughter's hair, she connected with the jeweled barrette. Everything was changing. Grant was gone, her little girl was growing up and Nick Bluestone might become her husband.

Morning brought a cool December breeze and a myriad of tangled emotions.

Elaina stood beside a row of pipe stalls, fenced enclosures that were attached to the barn, giving the horses the opportunity to venture outside.

This environment, she thought, could become her permanent home. The land, the country roads, the trees, the horses.

She turned to look at Kid. The young gelding had been watching her, inching forward whenever she pretended not to notice him.

"Did you eat already?" she asked.

Elaina had fed all the horses, a chore she'd taken upon herself. Since she'd spent a restless night tossing and turning, she'd headed for the barn at dawn, anxious for something to do.

"I brought a treat," she said, wondering if Kid could smell the carrots. She'd filled two plastic bags and stuffed them into her pockets, intending to offer the horses a snack after their morning meal.

She held out a carrot, and the gelding froze, refusing to approach her hand.

She waited a few minutes, but he didn't budge.

"All right. I'll just leave you alone, then." She turned her back and heard him snort. Kid reminded her of a neglected child. He craved affection, but didn't know how to accept it. And that, she realized, was exactly why Nick had purchased the ill-mannered gray.

Nick Bluestone was a patient, kindhearted man. He lent himself to those who needed him.

Elaina took a deep breath. Lexie needed him. That was a fact. She couldn't deny Nick's positive influence on her daughter. Lexie had begun to blossom in Oklahoma. Her daughter laughed and smiled and socialized with friends.

But should Elaina marry him for that reason, and that reason alone?

No, she shouldn't. Because eventually a tremulous marriage would take its toll on everyone, including Lexie.

Of course, she could stay in Oklahoma without accepting Nick's proposal. She could get an apartment in town, and Lexie could visit her uncle on the weekends. Nick would still be part of their lives.

Yet that wasn't what Grant had asked of his brother. He'd asked Nick to take his place, to become Elaina's husband and Lexie's full-time father.

But there had to be a part of her that wanted to marry Nick, a part of her that needed him, too. Otherwise it would never work.

What about companionship? She needed a friend, didn't she? A mate who wasn't looking for love? Someone who thought kindness and respect was enough to make a marriage work.

She closed her eyes, knowing her fate was sealed. She was going to marry him because it was the right thing to do, for Lexie, for herself and for Nick.

Five minutes later, Elaina entered the house through the back door, and nearly ran straight into Lexie, who tried to rush past her.

"What's the hurry? What's going on?" And why in the world was her daughter up so early on a Saturday morning?

"*Ap* asked me to feed the horses, and I want to get it done before Ryan gets here." She bounced in youthful anticipation. "All of us are working today. Starr, Ryan and me. *Ap* is getting everything ready for us."

Elaina closed the door, blocking the wind. They stood in the laundry room, the shelves stocked with cleaning supplies, a clump of towels piled on the washer. "Relax. I already fed the horses."

"You did?" Lexie blew a relieved sigh. "That's great, Mom. Thanks."

The girl adjusted the barrette in her hair, and Elaina smiled. The glittering rose just might become a permanent fixture. "So Ryan is finally making an appearance. I kept wondering when we would get to meet him."

"Me, too. I should probably go. I've got a lot of work to do."

And a teenage boy to impress, she thought. "That's fine. But I still need a second of your time." She moved closer, her smile fading. "I made a decision."

"You did?"

Lexie glanced up, and their eyes met—daughter to mother, young girl to woman. The look that passed between them was an expression only another female could read.

"You're going to marry him, aren't you?"

Suddenly Elaina's voice fought for silence. Once she said it, there would be no turning back. She would be making a commitment to a man she barely knew, changing the pattern, the familiarity of her life.

"Mom?"

"Yes. I'm going to marry him."

"It's what Daddy wanted," the girl reassured her.

"I know." Elaina forced a smile. She couldn't burden Lexie with her fears, with the anxiety of accepting Nick as her husband. "I'm okay with it. I'm sure it's what I should do."

Lexie bounced like a child again, her soulful wisdom gone. "Can I tell Starr?"

"Yes, but not until I tell Nick." Which Elaina assured her daughter would be soon. "Once Starr and Ryan get here, I'll come by the workshop to see if your uncle is free to talk."

"All right. I guess I should go." Lexie turned, then paused before she opened the door. "If you want me to wear a dress at the wedding, I will. As long as it's not one of those big, puffy ones."

"Oh, my." Wedding preparations hadn't crossed her mind, nor had formal attire, for herself or for Lexie.

"We'll see, okay?" She watched her daughter leave, nerves jumping and jangling in her stomach.

Elaina waited an hour, keeping herself busy in the process. She tidied the living room and did the laundry, and when the towels were neatly folded and put away, she reached for her coat.

On her way to the workshop, she passed a motorcycle parked by the side of the house. She continued walking, hoping she'd given Nick enough time to get the kids settled into their work.

Lexie and Starr glanced up as Elaina entered the building. Both girls shared the same bench, each performing a separate task. Lexie sent her a reassuring smile, and she thanked God for her daughter, for the child she loved with all her heart. Starr grinned, too, and she added another thanks for budding friendships.

Nick, seated at a sewing machine, seemed unaware of her presence, and a young man she could only assume was Ryan wielded a rawhide mallet.

He was a teenage heartthrob, all right, the kind of boy girls gathered in hallways to talk about. His long hair, banded into a ponytail, left the handsome angles of his face unframed, defining strong bones and a youthful dimple.

No doubt Lexie had developed an immediate crush. Between his striking appearance and the buildup Starr had given him, Ryan couldn't lose.

The rumble of the sewing machine stopped. Elaina moved farther into the room, and Nick looked up.

He came toward her, and she reminded herself to breathe. He wore an ensemble of faded denim, with silver bracelets glinting at his wrists. Did he sleep with his jewelry on? She had never seen him without it.

"Hi," he said. "Are you here to give us a hand?"

"No. I was wondering if you had a few minutes to spare. To talk."

"Sure." He met her gaze, then glanced quickly at Ryan. "Will you hold down the fort? Help the girls if they need anything?"

The boy nodded and smiled, his dimple engaging even deeper. "No problem."

Nick grabbed his jacket from behind a chair and ushered Elaina toward the door. She looked over her shoulder at Lexie, hoping for another boost of moral support, but her daughter was watching Ryan.

The moment they stepped outside, a small gust of wind snapped out of the sky, rattling leaves and blowing dirt into tiny dust devils.

"Where do you want to go?" he asked.

She jammed her hands into her pockets and connected with carrots. "To the barn." At the moment it seemed as good a place as any. And she still hadn't given the horses their treat.

The breezeway barn wasn't exactly warm, but Elaina took comfort in the greeting they received from the animals. Even Kid came toward the front of his stall, wary but curious.

Without saying anything to Nick, she removed the

plastic bags from her pockets and began distributing carrots, dividing them evenly. But when she reached Kid's hay crib, she snuck in a few extra bites.

Nick leaned against the wall, watching her. "I saw that," he said, sounding amused. "You're spoiling him."

She shrugged and caught his smile—that slightly crooked, extremely seductive smile. "He doesn't seem to think so," she noted, as Kid ignored the offering.

"Sure he does. He's just playing hard to get."

Unsure of what to do with the empty bags, she stuffed them back into her pockets. "Can we sit somewhere?" Because if they didn't, she feared her legs would give way. Suddenly her knees had turned to jelly.

"Of course." He recommended the feed room, so they took up residence on a bale of hay.

She glanced at her hands, feeling shy and uncomfortable. Starr and Lexie were probably faring better with Ryan. After all, they had youth in their corner. Elaina was too old for this kind of knee-weakening, heart-palpitating attraction.

And damn it, she had sex to worry about. A hot, steamy wedding night with her brother-in-law. Would they talk about it? Or would it just happen? The idea of sleeping with him made her nervous. Excited. Aroused. She imagined kissing his navel, sliding her tongue over that hidden tattoo.

"Elaina?"

She lifted her head, felt her nipples tighten. "What?"

"I thought you wanted to talk."

"I did. I do. I'm accepting your proposal," she said finally, agreeing to spend the rest of her life with her brother-in-law.

Six

The day had come. Elaina and Lexie were getting ready in the chapel's tiny dressing room, but Nick was too anxious to wait inside or chat with the guests who had arrived. Instead he strolled through a maze of trees, drawing comfort from Mother Earth.

The mountain air was cool and clean, the sky a deep, dark shade of blue. The temperature didn't seem cold enough for snow, but he suspected rain by nightfall.

He could see the chapel from where he was, so he stopped to admire its primitive beauty. Christmas lights twinkled on a timber fence, and a small steeple reached toward the heavens, topped with a rough-hewn cross. The multipaned windows reflected a kaleidoscope of colored glass, but overall, the tiny church was a simple clapboard structure, surrounded by God's green earth.

Nick felt closer to the Creator here, and he'd visited the chapel many times since his brother's murder, praying for the strength and guidance to fulfill the vow he'd made to Grant.

He inhaled the scent of evergreens, his heart filling with tears. He missed his brother desperately.

Take care of my family...the old way. Be the Comanche I should have been. Teach my daughter... protect my wife....

"I'm marrying Elaina today," he whispered back to the voice in his head, to the voice of his twin. Reaching into his pocket, he lifted the ring. It glinted in his hand, a slim circle of gold. "I'll treat her right, *bávi,* brother. I promise."

Nick stared at the ring. He wished he had the courage to tell her the truth about the night Grant had died, but he couldn't bear to relive that moment, to admit that he'd taken her husband away. So instead he would live with the burden and guilt, praying each night for forgiveness.

"Nick? Are you out here?"

"Yes," he answered, recognizing Tony Horn's voice. Emerging from the trees, he walked toward his boyhood friend.

The other man stood with his hands in his pockets, his shoulders hunched. "You okay?" he asked.

"Sure. Why wouldn't I be?"

Tony shrugged, flashing his half-cocked grin. "Oh, I dunno. Could be you're getting married this afternoon." He paused to make his point. "Nicky Bluestone is taking the final plunge. Never thought I'd see the day."

Nick shook his head. "We're not going to go through that again, are we?"

Tony reached into his pocket for a cigarette, then cupped his hand to light it. He blew smoke into the wind, his expression suddenly serious. "Truthfully, I'm glad you're falling for her."

"That's not how it is." Nick's pulse shot up his arm. The idea alone scared the hell out of him. He couldn't fall for Elaina, not in the way Tony meant. She would always belong to Grant. "It's my responsibility to marry my brother's wife."

"Your brother's *widow*. Remember that, Nicky. She's Grant's widow, but she's going to be your wife."

And Tony was trying to talk him into claiming Elaina, into taking her away from Grant, into loving a woman who would never really be his. "This won't be that kind of marriage. Not for either one of us."

"All right." The other man backed off. "But be happy, okay? Promise me that much."

Nick nodded. He knew his friend cared about him. They'd grown up together, with Grant laughing beside them, encouraging Tony's boyish shenanigans. "Deal. But I expect a promise in return."

"Sure. What?"

"That you won't sabotage the cabin tonight. No shaving cream in the bed or rice in the shower."

"Who me?" The legendary prankster widened his eyes, and they both laughed.

After a moment of silence, Tony checked his watch. "We should go. It's almost time."

They walked back to the chapel, and before they entered through a side door, Tony took one last hit off the cigarette. Looking around for a nonexistent ashtray, he extinguished it on the bottom of his boot.

Nick raised an eyebrow, and Tony grinned and shoved the butt into his pocket.

They took their places on the side of the altar, and Nick was glad the other man had agreed to stand up for him.

The chapel was peaceful and fragrant. A shimmering rainbow, a gift from the stained glass windows, dappled the rustic interior. Two gold candles and a bundle of sage burned at the altar. The minister waited at the pulpit, while a small gathering of friends found places in wooden pews.

Native American flute music played softly in the background, and Lexie came down the aisle. She placed a white candle between the others, then stood quietly on the other side of the altar. She looked pretty, Nick thought. Little Lexie in feminine attire, her smile young and bright.

The music didn't change, but Nick sensed the instant Elaina entered the chapel. A cashmere dress in a creamy beige hue clung to her curves. The neckline displayed a jeweled collar—tiny sparks catching the rainbow. Two glittering combs swept her hair away from her face. She didn't look like a traditional bride, but she was a vision wrapped in winter warmth. Her bouquet was a long, graceful sweep of orchids.

She stood beside him. He wanted to tell her how beautiful she was, but the minister began to speak, drawing Nick's gaze forward. He couldn't help but wonder if Elaina was thinking about her other wedding. She seemed shy and nervous. Her best friend hadn't been able to attend on such short notice, and Nick worried that she felt a little too alone. Truthfully, he wasn't sure if she'd even told her parents. They were in Switzerland for the holidays, skiing at a fancy resort.

The minister addressed them, and Nick turned toward his bride. The ceremony included an exchange of rings and a vow of forever. When the time came for a kiss, he leaned into her and touched her lips softly. She closed her stunning blue eyes, and he tasted the sweet, gentle warmth of a woman.

Afterward, they looked at each other, the chapel hushed. Side by side, they stepped forward to light the white candle, a gesture signifying the beginning of their life together.

Wax-scented smoke rose in the air. He took her hand and felt it tremble in his. It was done. They were married—two people whose hearts were beating much too fast.

Elaina assessed Nick's cabin. A modern kitchen, artfully disguised with rough-hewn cupboards, buzzed with feminine chatter. Children played on a flight of wooden stairs that led to a loft, and a small group of men, including Nick, gathered around a stone hearth, laughing and joking. Other guests milled around, their plates laden with second helpings. Lexie and Starr, bundled in winter coats, sat on the porch with Ryan and several other teenagers.

The atmosphere was definitely festive, Elaina thought. A casual, comfortable party.

Vera Horn managed to socialize while she worked. She seemed to be enjoying herself, whether she was adding more chicken to a platter or washing a greasy pan. She bustled about in a colorful cotton dress, her gray hair coiled in a tidy bun. Friendly eyes crinkled beneath wire-rimmed glasses.

Elaina was in the kitchen, icing a freshly baked cake. She didn't mind helping with the reception. It kept her from staring at Nick, from meeting his gaze across the room. They were just too aware of each other, and that made her nervous. They hadn't talked about making love, but spending the night together was on both their minds.

Vera moved in beside her. "This marriage was meant to be. You did the right thing."

"Thank you. Nick's a good man." She glanced up to find him watching her. He smiled, and her heart bounced against her breast. He was dressed all in black, silver bracelets shackling his wrists, a white orchid pinned to his lapel. She returned his smile, feeling like a fluttery schoolgirl.

Elaina finished icing the cake, having done her best to make it pretty. She knew he was still studying her, catching glimpses with those magnetic eyes. Sexy Nick, she thought. Stealing glances. It made her want him even more, a forbidden desire she couldn't seem to control.

"Yes. Nicky's a good boy. He always was." Vera patted her hand. "Come with me to the loft. I have something for you."

As they climbed the stairs, the older woman greeted the children, a handful of little Comanches with gap-toothed grins. The kids giggled and let the adults pass, their playtime of utmost importance.

Vera guided Elaina into a room with a small balcony. An impressive view offered trees, grassland and rocky peaks. A river flowed in the distance, a deep, dark body of water.

"It's beautiful here," Elaina said. The room was furnished with a queen-size spindle bed and an Indian blanket. Speckled logs decorated the walls, and a tiny fireplace waited for a flame.

Was this where she would sleep with Nick?

Vera opened the top drawer of a pine dresser. She removed a small bundle and sat on the edge of the bed. Elaina sat next her, and Vera unwrapped the cloth.

"This is for a serenity bath," the older woman said, presenting a colorful gathering of herbs, flower petals and leaves. "After everyone is gone, fill the tub and then sprinkle this into the water. The scent will draw your mind into quiet passageways."

"Thank you." It was a beautiful gesture, Elaina thought, an offering to a nervous bride. "I do need to relax."

"And someday you'll prepare your daughter for her husband. You'll give her a serenity bath."

"Yes, I will." She touched the bundle, the aroma sweet and inviting. "Will you tell me what everything is?"

"You should recognize the ingredients. They're plants you often see."

This was a lesson, Elaina realized, from a wise old grandmother. She fingered the mixture, allowing silky petals and green leaves to fall between her fingers. "Roses and mint," she said, aware that Vera had given her a simple gift from nature—things she could grow or buy from a florist.

Vera nodded. "What else?"

She lifted a dried herb. "It smells familiar. Like a tea I've drunk. Chamomile."

"Good. What about the bigger leaves?"

"I'm not sure." But they, too, seemed familiar.

"They're from a garden violet. They provide vitamin C." A teasing smile softened a strong, sun-burnished face. "A new bride needs her vitamins, especially on her wedding night."

"Are you trying to tell me something about the man I married?" Elaina met Vera's gaze, and they both laughed.

A second later Elaina's eyes misted. She had always longed for a mentor, an older woman to guide her. Her mother had never been available for quiet conversation or feminine pampering.

She reached out to hug Vera, and they embraced. "Thank you. This means so much to me."

"You're welcome." The older lady closed the bundle. "Now let's serve the cake. In no time, the guests will leave, and then you can be alone with your husband."

Yes, Elaina thought, taking a deep breath. Nick Bluestone. My gorgeous brother-in-law. My Comanche husband.

Elaina emerged from the tub, her skin smooth and scented. The herbal bath had soothed her nerves, but she was still aware of her body, of the forbidden hunger running through her veins.

She dried with a thick towel, and then studied the nightgown she'd chosen to wear—a slim-cut design void of lace or fancy adornments. The matching robe lay beside the gown in a pool of blue silk.

Her panties were a wisp of material, nearly the same tone as her flesh. Her bare nipples tingled, already anticipating Nick's touch.

She dressed and left her hair the way it was, pinned in a loose, hasty chignon. She'd lifted it off her shoulders for the bath, and now she liked the way it looked. Besides, she wanted Nick to release the pins.

Tonight was a fantasy she couldn't deny. Tonight she would lie naked with her Comanche husband.

Elaina glanced at the tub, and wondered if Vera had a remedy for guilt, if there were plants and flowers that would make sleeping with Nick seem less forbidden.

Husband or not, he was still Grant's brother. And yes, in the old days brothers lent each other their wives. But this was modern times, and she felt sinful for wanting Nick, even with a license between them.

Don't feel guilty for being attracted to your new husband, she told herself a moment later. Nick Bluestone was a good man.

Clinging to that thought, she belted her robe and entered the bedroom.

Nick sat on an Indian blanket in front of the fireplace. He'd removed his shirt and boots, but he still sported the black trousers he'd worn to the chapel.

He turned toward her, and Elaina nearly staggered. His chest was wide and solid, the color of polished copper, but the scars were a testimony of sadness, pale and raised. She didn't have to ask how he'd acquired them. She knew.

He'd cut himself. He'd mourned his brother the Comanche way.

Heaven help her, but she could almost feel the knife, the blade slicing his skin.

"What's wrong?" he asked.

"Nothing." She couldn't admit what seeing his scars had done to her. Suddenly she wanted to cry, but tears would only remind them of the husband she'd lost, of the brother he'd bled for. And there were enough reminders already. They were married because of Grant.

"I'm fine," she said.

He motioned to the fireplace. "I thought a fire might be nice."

Elaina nodded. The woodsy aroma of burning logs filled the small room. Outside, the sky had opened up, showering rain upon the earth. She could hear it slashing against the windows.

"Are you sure you're okay?"

"Yes." Part of his tattoo was visible, just enough to send her eyes drifting lower. She couldn't discern the design, but she imagined putting her mouth there and making his stomach muscles quiver.

"Then sit with me, Elaina."

She knelt on the blanket, and he handed her a steaming mug.

"I always crave hot chocolate when it rains," he said. "I couldn't resist."

"Thank you." The drink tasted rich and sweet, the marshmallows melting on her tongue. "I really like this cabin." So isolated, she thought. A rustic haven tucked away in the mountains, a retreat for lovers.

"I was worried Tony might booby-trap the place. His pranks are harmless, but I wasn't in the mood for jokes. Not tonight."

Because tonight was serious, Elaina thought. The vow they'd taken, the rain, the anticipated sex—all of it was serious. "Do you think Lexie made it back okay? I hope she remembers to call."

"They left before the rain started. But if she doesn't call soon, you can try to reach her. We'll wait until someone answers the phone at Starr's house."

We'll wait. She understood what Nick meant. They wouldn't make love until they knew her daughter was safe. "She hasn't spent the night at a friend's house in years. After Grant died, she stayed close to me."

"I know. But it's time for her to spread her wings a little. Don't worry, *cueh.* She'll be fine."

Cueh. Elaina placed her cup on the stone ledge of the fireplace. Nick was watching her, a red-and-gold flame bathing him in a warm glow. "Is that a Comanche word?"

"Yes."

"What does it mean?"

"Wife," he said, his gaze locked with hers.

Or sister-in-law, she realized, struggling to catch her breath. In the Comanche dialect they were one and the same. And coming from Nick, the word sounded soft and erotic.

The phone rang, jarring Elaina's thoughts. She jumped up and rushed to answer it.

"Hi, Mom. It's me." Lexie's voice came over the receiver. "We just got back. It's raining."

"I know. Here, too." She glanced out the window. "Are you okay, sweetie?"

"Sure. We rented a movie, and we're going to make popcorn."

"That sounds fun. Enjoy yourself, and I'll see you tomorrow."

"Okay. Tell *Ap* I said hi."

"I will." They exchanged a warm goodbye, and Elaina hung up the phone. Nick stood behind her. She could feel him there, tall and quiet.

She turned to face him. "Lexie said hi. They're in for the night."

"Good. I knew she'd be fine." Nick set his gaze directly on hers. "And now it's just us. We're all alone."

"Yes." With a fire glowing and an empty bed beside them.

Their conversation ceased, and the storm intensified, rumbling with thunder.

He moved closer. His eyes were deep and intense, and a strand of hair fell across his forehead in an inky-black line. He looked dark and mysterious. She had the wicked notion to unzip his trousers, to explore the partially hidden tattoo.

"I want to touch you, Elaina. I want to put my hands all over you."

Her knees nearly buckled. His admission, those

simple, honest words, had her struggling to stand upright. "I want to touch you, too."

Nick untied her robe. "Then we'll take turns." The robe fell to the floor, and the straps on her nightgown slipped down, over her shoulders. "But I get to go first. I get to make you crazy."

He undressed her while they kissed, while their mouths came together as slick and silky as the rain. The sensation hugged her body like a smooth, satin ribbon, and she gave in to the feeling, to the heat that made her want this man.

Her new husband. Her brother-in-law. Suddenly none of that mattered. He was big and powerful, and she needed him.

He explored her, his hands and his mouth questing. Elaina watched him, her pulse as rhythmic as the night.

He licked her nipples, stroked her belly, and then eased her against the footboard. She reached back and grabbed hold of the wooden spindles. He still wore his trousers, and she was naked, standing before him like an eager sacrifice.

"Do you know what I'm going to do to you?" he asked.

"Yes." She knew, and she had no desire to stop him. She wanted to feel his mouth pressed against her, his tongue warm and wet and slick.

He didn't disappoint. He dropped to his knees, and then ravaged her. There was no other way to describe what was happening. She bucked on contact, fast and hard, still gripping the bedpost for support.

This was, Elaina thought, the sexiest moment of her life. As willing as she was, the forbidden edge had returned. She shouldn't crave him, but she did. She hungered for every throaty pant, every breathless moan.

He looked up, and she saw sparks in his eyes—those dark, penetrating eyes. He was strong and demanding, relentlessly male, determined to pull her into the flame, the fire that seemed to be burning all around them.

Even when she climaxed, he didn't stop. He kept kissing and licking, tasting her over and over.

He wanted more. She knew that. He wanted to take her as far as she could go. He wanted to brand her flesh, her mind, her emotions. Tonight was theirs—the jagged mountains, the driving rain, the unbridled sex.

She struggled for balance, but the next climax slammed straight into her heart, piercing part of her soul. The feeling, the bone-deep sensation, thrilled and terrified her all at once. Losing her breath, she shuddered, gasping between urgent sobs and reckless sighs.

And when it ended, she swayed, her body trembling.

Nick came to his feet, and she blinked, focusing on every feature—the slant of his cheekbones, slash of his eyebrows, cut of his jaw. He kissed her, and she tasted herself on his lips—a blend of sex, sweet sin and seduction.

Still aroused, Elaina nibbled on his earlobe. "It's my turn," she whispered. To lick and tease and drive him crazy. She unzipped his trousers, and he made a rough sound.

"Just don't go too far, okay? I'm not sure how long I can hold on."

His admission gave her power. She smiled—a smile as slow and easy as the way she intended to caress him. Yes, she would push him to the brink of insanity, but she would do it gently. "I promise to give you a chance, Nick."

He sucked in a barely controlled breath. "That almost sounded like a dare."

Was it? She couldn't be sure. If she was challenging him, then she wasn't doing it deliberately. She just wanted to touch him, to make his heartbeat stagger.

Nick's heartbeat wouldn't stabilize. He felt it banging against his chest, pounding like a native drum. Elaina sat on the edge of the bed, and her face was eye-level with his zipper—his open fly.

It was, he thought, strangely erotic to stand before her, fully aroused and anticipating her touch.

She tugged on his pants, just enough to expose his navel. And when she kissed his belly, a warm shiver slid up and down his spine.

"Tell me about your tattoo," she said. "Tell me what it means."

For a moment he only stared, his mind blank. But then he realized she was intrigued by the bold design on his stomach.

"It's a pattern associated with the Comanche Thunderbird." He took her finger and traced the thick blue lines. "This represents the color of its body, like a thundercloud. And the red—" he guided her over a zigzag pattern that cut across his navel "—is the marking that extends from the bird's heart to its wings." And the tattoo had been inked in a primitive fashion, using a sharp thorn instead of a needle to pierce his skin.

She kissed his belly again, making his muscles jump.

"This looks like an arrow," she said, commenting on another shape in the tribal design.

"It is. The Thunderbird carries arrows in its talons."

"Does he make thunder?"

"Yes." Nick caressed her cheek, and they both listened to the downpour falling from the sky. "He creates the storm. He blinks flashing eyes to produce lightning and flaps enormous wings to make thunder. Rain comes from the river he carries on his back." Nick glanced at the window, at the mist fogging the glass. "He's out there now. Or at least his spirit is."

Elaina looked up, her eyes as blue as a gemstone. "And you made peace with him."

"I tried to." Because Nick needed to be part of the elements, allowing thunderstorms to live inside him. "The Comanche used to fear thunder and lightning. It was dangerous, and it gave them no power."

She removed his pants, taking his briefs with them. When he was naked, she teased the tip of his sex, and he buried his hands in her hair.

"It gives you power," she said.

They didn't speak after that. She took him into her mouth, and he removed the pins from her hair. The chestnut mass fell in thick waves over her shoulders. He toyed with each silky strand, twining them around his fingers, watching them shimmer in his hands.

He stroked her hair while she stroked him. The sensation was smooth and sexy, like floating naked in a river, sun-dappled water bathing his skin.

Her mouth was warm and wet. Feeling intoxicated, he slipped into a state of drugged arousal. And for a second, for one desperate second, he had the masculine urge to increase the rhythm, to cup her face and push himself deeper.

"Cueh," he whispered, his voice rough. "You have to stop."

"No, Nick. Not yet." She licked her way up his body, running her hands over his skin, stimulating him even more. And when she finally met him eye-to-eye, he nudged her onto the bed, and they both went crazy.

Heat. Urgency.

They rumpled the blanket as they rolled, mouths coming together in a searing kiss. He sucked on her tongue; she nipped his bottom lip. They rubbed against each other, loin against loin.

Nick took her nipples into his mouth, grazing her with his teeth. Her breasts were round and full, her skin creamy and smooth, so much paler than his. She smelled of flower petals and mint, of feminine lust and winter storms.

He wanted to tell her how long it had been since he'd made love, how long he had waited for her, but he couldn't find the words. Nor could he bear to say them out loud, to admit how much he needed her.

"I can't wait, Elaina." Still straddling her, he reached for the dresser and opened the top drawer, where he'd scattered a handful of condoms.

She watched him tear open the foil, and he studied her—this woman he had vowed to marry. Her hair, mussed from his fingers, fanned against a pillow. And her lips, swollen from the taste of his, were slightly parted.

They kissed again, and he entered her, full hilt. She wrapped her legs around him, and he moved.

The primitive dance. The fast, intensifying motion. He pushed deeper, and she rose to meet him, stroke for wild stroke.

Rain pounded against the windows, and when she closed around him like a damp fist, he could have sworn lightning streaked across the bed, flashing in a jagged white light.

Their power, he thought as they climaxed in each other's arms. Their incredible, soul-clenching power.

Seven

Morning arrived in a dark gray mist. Water drizzled from the sky, like silent, lonely tears from heaven.

Elaina sat up and reached for her robe. The fire no longer glowed, and the golden warmth it had provided was long gone. All that was left was charred wood.

And a beautiful man beside her.

She turned to study Nick. He slept peacefully, the blanket draped around his hips. With his features still and his eyes closed, he looked just like Grant, except for the scars marring his chest and the sterling bracelets glinting at his wrists.

She reached out to caress his cheek, then felt her hand shake. She drew back quickly, her heart pounding against her breast.

Heaven help her. She was actually afraid of touching him, afraid of the electricity, the surge of lightning that had sparked between them last night.

How could their lovemaking have been that powerful? That intense? They barely knew each other.

With a sleepy moan, Nick stretched and opened his eyes. And when their gazes connected, he blinked and smiled.

"Hi," he said, pulling himself to an upright position.

Elaina tried not to look, but the blanket slipped, exposing his tattooed navel and the shadow of hair below it. They'd slept naked, wrapped in each other's arms most of the night.

"Hi." Her greeting was but a whisper, a barely spoken word.

He turned toward the window. The shutters were open, bringing in the misty gray light. "It's hardly raining anymore."

Elaina nodded, unsure of what to do. Her first morning-after with Grant had been easy, a natural step in their relationship. They'd dated, spent months getting to know each other. But Nick was more or less a stranger.

He turned back and caught her expression. "Elaina, what's wrong?"

"Nothing," she said much too softly.

His chest heaved with a laden breath. And when he dragged a hand through his hair and tamed the rebellious strands falling across his forehead, she held her breath. He was so beautiful, so dangerously handsome.

"I can tell you're worried about something. Is it us? Is it what happened last night?"

She nodded, wondering if he'd felt it, too. The power. The lightning. The moment their bodies had become one.

"We're married," he said. "We didn't do anything wrong."

"I know." Her eyes began to water. "But I shouldn't be this attracted to you. It shouldn't be like this, and certainly not this soon. Two weeks ago you proposed to me, and last night I couldn't take my hands off you."

He adjusted the blanket. "Why wouldn't you be attracted to me? I look like Grant. I'm his identical twin."

"That's not why I slept with you."

Nick moved closer, praying she wasn't going to cry. He never knew what to do when women cried. "I don't understand what's troubling you."

"We barely know each other," she said. "We're not friends, not in the true sense of the word. Grant and Lexie are all we have in common."

He couldn't argue her point, because she was right. The vows they'd taken yesterday didn't make them friends. That had to come from the heart. "Then we'll get to know each other, okay? We'll talk. We'll date. We'll do what couples do."

They sat quietly then, and he realized how difficult

his solution was. Suddenly neither one of them could think of anything to say.

Nick shifted his weight, stirring the mattress. Why hadn't he spent quality time alone with her, forming the friendship she needed?

Because he'd always steered clear of emotional intimacy. He was thirty-six years old and he'd never had a live-in lover. Girlfriends came and went in his life.

But now he was married, damn it, and his wife deserved more than just sex. Of course, it had been incredible sex, he reminded himself.

"Why was last night so good?" she asked, as if she'd read his mind. "Why did we make each other feel that way?"

"Because we're human. And sensuality is part of our nature." He exhaled a rough breath, wishing this wasn't so awkward. "And let's face it, neither one of us has had sex in a long time. We were bound to go a little crazy."

Elaina tilted her head. "I thought you had a lot of lovers."

A lot? Nick wasn't sure how many that meant, and he wasn't about to analyze it with a number.

"Why haven't you had sex recently?" she asked, her head still cocked at a curious angle.

Uncomfortable, he frowned, cursing himself for letting that slip. "I just haven't."

She narrowed her watery eyes. "That doesn't make sense. I mean, you of all people. The playboy who sampled the flavor of the month."

"I'm not a playboy. And I didn't switch lovers every month. That was just a joke between Grant and me. A stupid guy-thing we started saying when we were kids. I experimented before he did, and he used to bug me about it." Why in the hell were they having this conversation anyway? He was married now—to her.

"Why won't you tell me how long it's been?"

"Fine. You want to know. I'll tell you." He grabbed his pants off the floor and shoved them on as quickly as he could. "I've been celibate for over two years."

Once again, silence bounced between them. He stood near the fireplace in a pair of wrinkled trousers, and she sat on the bed in a silky blue robe, staring up at him.

"Oh, Nick."

"What was I supposed to do? Sleep with other women? I made a vow to marry you. It wouldn't have been right." He shook his head. "And stop looking at me like I'm some sort of martyr. It wasn't easy. There were times I wanted to cheat. More times than I care to admit." He hadn't functioned well without sex, without the basic, primal need that made him a man.

"This is so confusing. I feel so strange inside." She drew the blanket around her. "What you did, Nick. What you gave up. It was an honorable thing to do."

"Please don't make a big deal out of it." Because he wasn't as honorable as he seemed. He was keeping a horrible secret—the truth about the night Grant had died. "Let's just give ourselves some time to get used to our situation." He moved toward the bed and sat next to her. "We consummated our marriage too quickly. We let things happen too fast. So why don't we slow down from now on?"

She met his gaze. "No more sex?"

He nodded, wishing he could hold her. "Not until you're comfortable about all of this. I can't bear to see you cry every morning."

Her eyes filled up even more. "I might not know you very well, but I like you."

Nick smiled. "I like you, too." And he wouldn't disrespect her by demanding his conjugal rights, not when she was struggling to accept him as her lover. "But do you think it would be okay if we shared a room? I mean, you don't mind sleeping next to me, do you?"

"No," she said softly. "I don't mind at all."

Elaina sat on the arena fence, watching her daughter's second horseback-riding lesson. Lexie looked good in the saddle, proud and sure of herself. She took the gelding through each gait with comfort and ease.

Nick climbed the rail and sat next to Elaina. "She's a natural," he said.

"She certainly seems happy." And Elaina couldn't begin to describe how that made her feel. Lexie's hair was blowing in the wind, the ebony strands shining beneath a silver sky. The young girl was part of the elements, she thought, part of the air and the grass and the trees.

"It's the Comanche in her." Nick smiled like the father he was becoming. "She was born to ride. She should have her own horse, though. None of mine are quite right for her."

Elaina studied the man who had given her daughter the gift of contentment. Today he wore faded jeans and scuffed leather boots, a denim jacket buttoned at his waist.

"Thank you," she said.

"For what?"

"For caring so much."

"She's my brother's child, and that makes her mine. In my heart, I helped conceive her. Lexie belongs to me, too."

"I know." Their gazes locked, caught in a reflection of tenderness. She had been sleeping beside Nick for the past two nights, but they hadn't caressed or kissed. He had offered to get to know her first, and she knew he meant to keep that promise.

A horse snorted, and Elaina turned to see Lexie coming toward them. The young girl smiled and reined in the gelding. He stopped on command.

"Nick says you're doing great, that you're a natural."

"Really?" Lexie glanced at her uncle for approval.

"Yeah, really." He grinned. "You're a Comanche, baby. Through and through. Our ancestors ruled the plains."

"Did my dad ride?"

"He sure did. An old cowboy in the neighborhood

taught both of us. Of course, your dad didn't ride much when he got older. He focused on school instead, on getting a scholarship to college."

"Daddy was smart."

Nick nodded. "Smarter than me, that's for sure. Did he ever tell you about our family name? About how it got to be Bluestone?"

Lexie shook her head. "Daddy never talked about the Indian stuff."

No, Elaina thought, he never did. Grant had kept his heritage locked inside. And when he died, he gave his brother permission to share it with Lexie, to teach her who she was and where she'd come from.

"Then I'll tell you, Miss Bluestone," Nick said to his niece. "But first you've got to unsaddle that horse. He won't work as well for you next time if you let him stand around too much."

Within ten minutes, the tack was returned to the barn and the stocky gelding was cooling down in the arena, rolling and enjoying his freedom. He had an impressive disposition, but Elaina was still infatuated with Kid, the flashy gray with the rebellious attitude.

Rather than remain at the fence rail, Elaina and Nick sat on a picnic bench in the backyard. Lexie, eager to hear what her uncle had to say, sat across from them.

"Before we received land allotments, the Comanche used to live on a reservation," Nick began. "And it was then that my great-great-grandfather was given the name Bluestone. I'm not sure why his Comanche name wasn't used. Either he chose to keep it a secret or it just didn't translate well. But either way, he was registered as Bluestone. And according to the federal government, the father's name became the family surname."

"Why Bluestone?" Lexie asked.

"Because he always wore a blue stone around his neck. Bright blue." Nick turned to look at Elaina. "Like your mother's eyes."

Self-conscious, she glanced away. Nick had been gazing directly into her eyes. And whenever he did that, her knees weakened, making her feel like an inexperienced schoolgirl.

Lexie scooted to the edge of the bench. "What kind of stone was it?"

Nick turned back to his niece. "I don't know. But it must have been special to him. He was proud of his English name."

"I like it, too. Don't you, Mom?"

"Yes." And she had married two men from the Bluestone family. "I think it's pretty."

Nick looked at her again, and she wondered if he'd always been partial to blue eyes.

The following evening Nick left his workshop and entered the house through the back door. He heard the clatter of pots and pans, the sound of running water. It still felt a little strange to have a woman nearby, to have her preparing meals and washing dishes. But he liked it, too. The house always smelled good. Homey and warm. Or sexy, he thought, when Elaina's perfume drifted through the air.

He headed for the kitchen. Elaina stood at the counter, putting the finishing touches on some sort of casserole. Nick didn't even know he owned a casserole dish. She'd probably found it buried in a cupboard, covered with dust.

"Hi," he said.

"Hi." She glanced up and smiled. "Long day at the office?"

He grinned back at her. "Yeah, something like that." He'd put in twelve hours today. He supplied a local Western store with custom accessories, and he had a last-minute order due before Christmas. Brushing his hands on his dye-stained jeans, he realized he needed a shower.

"It's just us tonight," she said.

"Really? Where's Lexie?"

Elaina turned to place the casserole in the oven. "Starr's grandparents took the girls to the mall. More Christmas shopping, I guess."

"That's nice." Lexie was certainly blossoming, Nick thought. And Starr, boy-crazy Starr, was turning out to be a good friend. But same-sex friends were easier to establish than the kind he and Elaina were working on. Men and women didn't always connect on the same level.

"How long before dinner is ready?" he asked.

"Twenty minutes or so. But I probably made too

much. I started the meal before Lexie was invited to go out."

"That's okay. There's always leftovers." Nick shifted his stance. How was he supposed to make friends with Elaina when he was keeping a secret from her? She deserved to know the truth about the night Grant had died.

But I can't tell her, he thought. God forgive me, but I can't bear to say the words out loud.

Feeling anxious, he ran a hand through his hair. "I'm going to take a quick shower."

He turned to leave, but she stopped him. "Nick?"

"Yes?"

"How do you like your steak?"

His heart bumped his chest. On the night Grant had died, they'd eaten at a steak house, two brothers out to have a good time. Grant had ordered filet mignon, rare, with a bottle of imported beer.

"Medium," he said, unnerved by the painful memory. There were always reminders, simple things that took him back to that night.

Nick entered the master bathroom and shed his clothes. Standing in the narrow stall, he let the water pummel his body.

Less than five minutes later, he stepped out of the shower, dried quickly and wrapped a towel around his waist. The mirror was fogged, so he wiped his hand across it, leaving an uneven streak.

He went through his regular grooming routine, and then stopped to take a rough breath.

The man in the glass looked like Grant. His face was dark and angular, his shorn hair combed straight back.

"I'm sorry, *bávi,*" he whispered. "I should have listened to you that night." And now you're gone, he thought. I didn't listen, and now you're gone.

With a familiar ache, Nick turned away from the mirror. He couldn't change the past, but he could secure Elaina and Lexie's future, just the way Grant had asked him to. He could be the best husband and father possible.

After zipping up a pair of freshly laundered jeans, he pulled a sweatshirt over his head. Because the hardwood floors were cold this time of year, he covered his feet with a pair of wool-lined moccasins.

A pleasant aroma drifted through the house. Elaina was moving between the kitchen and the dining room, setting the table.

"I'll do that," Nick said, announcing his presence.

She handed him their plates and silverware. "Thanks. The steaks are about done."

Nick studied the table. Something was missing.

Candles, he decided. After all, he and Elaina were newlyweds, dining alone for the first time. Tonight the scarred wood needed a touch of warmth. He retrieved a pair of buckhorn candleholders, realizing that was the best he could do.

As he lit the second wick, she came into the dining room, carrying the casserole between two potholders.

"Oh," she said. "That's pretty."

Nick smiled. He wanted to please her, to make her glad she'd married him. "Do you want wine with dinner?" he asked.

"Okay. But just a little."

She placed the steaming casserole on a metal trivet, a culinary accessory that had belonged to his grandmother. Just like the ancient baking dish, he realized. Suddenly the tiny blue pattern seemed familiar.

While Nick collected two glasses and a bottle of chardonnay, Elaina finished bringing the meal to the table.

They sat across from each other, candlelight flickering between them.

Nick reached for his fork. In place of lettuce, she'd prepared a cucumber salad smothered in a creamy dressing, and the casserole, he'd discovered, was a cheesy vegetable medley. Elaina never cooked anything plain. Even his steak was garnished with mushrooms, his potato one of those twice-baked numbers.

"This is great," he said.

"Thank you. I like to cook."

He grinned. "And I like to eat. So I guess that means we're the perfect couple."

She laughed a little. "Do you think so?"

Nick's teasing smile fell. Clearly they were struggling to have a real conversation. "We're not getting to know each other very well, are we?"

"It's only been four days."

"Yeah." And three restless nights of sleeping beside her, of wishing he could hold her, feel her body next to his.

"Why don't you tell me about your family," she said. "That's a good way for me to get to know you."

He wasn't sure what to say, considering his family had belonged to Grant, too. "Where should I start?"

"How about with your mother?"

Of course, he thought. His wayward mother. Pamela Bluestone always triggered curiosity. "She left when we were eleven."

"Grant told me she was moving to Florida to marry a man neither of you liked. So rather than go with her, you stayed with your grandmother."

"And that's all he said?" The same fabrication he'd told Lexie?

"Yes, but I didn't press the issue. I didn't ask him to expound."

Surprised, Nick sat quietly for a moment. "Why not?"

"Because I knew he wasn't comfortable talking about it. And since my mother has been married quite a few times, I'm aware of how difficult it can be to have a step-father."

"I see," he said. Apparently there had been something

missing in her childhood, too. The city girl with the well-to-do family. He'd suspected as much.

"Are you going to tell me about your mother?" she asked.

"Yeah, but sometime you've got to tell me about yours. After all, this getting-to-know-each-other stuff involves both of us."

For an instant he thought she was going to refuse. She glanced away, then challenged his gaze a second later. "All right," she said. "I suppose that's only fair. But you've met my mother, so you have an advantage."

He lifted an eyebrow. Sure, he'd seen her mom, first at Grant's wedding and then at his funeral. "I barely spoke to her. And we're not in competition, are we, Elaina? Whose mother was worse?"

"No, of course not. I'm sorry. I suppose that's the reason I avoided this conversation with Grant."

He backed down, realizing how painful this was for her. Being in the dark about Grant's family, as well as agreeing to talk about her own.

"Our mother's name was Pamela," he said, pulling himself into the past. "But she wasn't leaving to get married. True, there was a man from Florida, but he wasn't going to marry her."

Elaina cocked her head. "Then why did Grant say that?"

"To protect himself, maybe. To pretend our mom didn't abandon us. To blame her boyfriend instead of her." Nick held Elaina's gaze. "I don't know for sure. I just know that he cried when she left. And he started hating who he was and where he came from."

"You mean being poor?"

"And Indian."

Elaina closed her eyes. She should have known. She should have sensed that there was more to Grant than his fear of being stereotyped, than his need to rise above poverty. He'd lied to her, and she'd let it happen, never questioning the way he chose to live his life or raise their daughter.

"We didn't have a clue who our daddy was," Nick said as Elaina opened her eyes. "Mom dropped out of high school and started running with a wild crowd, and that's when she got pregnant." Frowning, he cut into his steak, the knife scraping his plate. "By the time Grant and I were in kindergarten, she was working at a cocktail lounge. This little dive on the edge of town."

"She wasn't abusive, was she?" Elaina asked, desperate for answers. She needed to know more about both of the men she had married.

"No, but she still wasn't cut out to be a mother. She made promises she never kept. Promises that meant the world to Grant." Nick laughed a little, the sound broken and bitter. "She kept saying that we were going to be rich someday. She'd meet a nice man, and he'd buy us a big, fancy house in the city."

Elaina's eyes misted, but because she couldn't bear to cry in front of Nick, she blinked away the tears. Those promises had been made to him, too.

"But when Prince Charming finally came along, she left without us. The guy was rich, but he wasn't respectable. She didn't date the kind of men who would raise someone else's children. She had been fooling herself as much as she'd been fooling us."

"I'm sorry, Nick."

He stared at his food. "Truthfully, there was less turmoil after she was gone. When Mom was around, people were always gossiping about her." Opening his hands, he made a wide gesture. "All of us lived here. Me, Grant, Grandma, Uncle Louie and Mom. But the house was just a shack, shabby and run-down. Grant and I slept on a mattress in the living room, and Mom was always hogging the bathroom, fixing her hair and doing her makeup, more like a big sister than a mother."

"And what about your grandma and Uncle Louie?"

"Grandma cooked and cleaned and chased after Louie. Loony Louie. That's what people called him. He was a handful. A grown man with no common sense."

"He was mentally challenged?"

"Yes, but he wasn't born that way. It happened later, when he was in his twenties. He was fixing a leak in the roof and fell off and hit his head. The injury created a permanent change in his mental state, and since Grandma was his older sister, she took responsibility for him after their parents died." Nick sighed. "We weren't the only poor folks around here, but we were the ones everybody talked about. Mom flirted with half the men in town, and Uncle Louie stole candy from the five-and-dime. That kind of stuff doesn't make you popular."

And the picture he painted broke her heart. An exhausted grandma, a brain-damaged great-uncle and a self-centered mother who had left them all behind. That was Nick and Grant's family.

"What happened to Uncle Louie?"

"He died when Grant and I were in high school. He was sixty years old, but he still seemed like a kid."

Elaina didn't respond. Instead she waited for Nick to tell her how Uncle Louie had died. She could see the memory in his eyes, like moonlight shimmering on an ebony sea.

"Louie loved snow, and whenever we'd get enough to play in, he'd bug us to make snow angels." With a slight pause, Nick glanced out the window. "One morning he decided to sneak outside and surprise us with angels all over the yard. He was out there for hours in his pajamas, just soaked to the bone. He got sick and ended up with pneumonia. Grandma said the angels must have wanted him."

Neither spoke after that. They finished their meal in silence, the table still laden with food, the candles still dancing with fire.

And at that moment Elaina felt a tender connection to Nick. A deeper understanding of who he was and why he'd remained close to home. Apparently he'd felt the need to present a new image to the community, proving he was a man worthy of admiration and respect—something Elaina intended to give him.

Eight

While Lexie slept the morning away, Nick and Elaina sat across from each other in the living room. He laced the edges of a custom-ordered belt, and she dominated the sofa with her beadwork, a small stack of reference books beside her.

Nick studied her through appreciative eyes. She wore a matching robe over lavender pajamas, and her hair fell in loose chestnut waves. The curtains were open, bathing her in a pale light.

Pretty, he thought. Sleek and womanly.

She looked up, and he focused on the belt, hoping he hadn't gotten caught staring. He'd watched her sleep throughout portions of the night, mesmerized by each soft, shallow breath.

"Who taught you to do beadwork?" she asked.

He brought his gaze back to hers. "No one. I learned from those books."

"Really? I thought maybe your grandmother taught you."

"No. She rarely had time for crafts. Besides, in the old days, sewing wasn't considered a particularly manly thing to do, and Grandma lived by most of those gender rules. She wouldn't have taught her grandsons to do woman's work."

Elaina smiled. "That must be why you never learned to cook."

He grinned. "You got me there. And Grant, too. He was lousy in the kitchen."

She nodded, her smile fading. "I miss him so much."

"I know. Me, too." In the early days, the Comanche didn't speak freely of the dead, but that was a tradition Nick couldn't adhere to. Saying his brother's name out loud helped keep the memories alive.

They worked in silence for the next few minutes, the Christmas tree filling the room with a fresh scent. Strands of tiny white lights twinkled on each branch, blinking like playful stars.

"So how are you doing?" he asked, motioning to her beadwork. Elaina had designed a snowflake pattern for her rosettes, choosing iridescent beads in shades of silver, pearl-white and blue. They were her contribution to the Christmas ornaments.

"Fine." She adjusted the embroidery hoop that secured the deerskin. "I enjoy doing woman's work."

And he enjoyed having his wife nearby.

Cueh, he thought. Wife. He'd already called her that, but he couldn't bring himself to say it again. That term aroused him now, conjuring images of their lovemaking, of Elaina naked beneath him.

He stared at the unfinished belt on his lap. He couldn't stop thinking about that night—the fire, the rain, the silky warmth between her thighs.

"Will you show me how to do the edge?"

"I'm sorry. What?" He lifted his gaze and slammed straight into hers. She'd been watching him, and he was skimming past an arousal, his body tight.

"The edge." She lifted the deerskin, displaying the rosette. "I don't know how to finish it."

"Oh, yeah. Sure."

He left his work on the chair and sat next to her. Single-bead edging. He searched his befuddled brain to remember how it was done. At the moment he couldn't think straight, and even the simplest project seemed complicated.

He could smell the fragrance of her skin, the light floral mist. Her perfumes and powders cluttered his bathroom. The feminine bottles, he thought, the cut crystal and smooth glass.

She waited, her lips slightly parted. And now he wanted to kiss her, lick and touch and taste.

Think, he told himself. Damn it all to hell. Think.

"Take one bead," he said. "And pass the needle from the front side of the leather. Below the edge, like this." He demonstrated the technique, explaining as he went. "Bring the needle back through the bead and pull it tight."

She watched with rapt attention, leaning into him. It would be so easy, he thought, to turn his head and nuzzle her hair, whisper something erotic in her ear.

Much too distracted, he jabbed himself with the needle.

The word that rushed out of his mouth was a harsh, vile curse.

"Sorry." Feeling coarse and ungentlemanly, he handed her the beadwork.

"That's okay. Believe me, I've heard that word before."

Maybe, but he didn't normally say it in mixed company. "I'm still sorry."

They looked at each other, and Nick's pulse pounded in an unspeakable place. He moved away, just a little, so their knees weren't touching. "Do you understand how to do the edge?"

"I think so."

She slipped a bead onto the needle, and he examined her work.

The rosette actually shimmered like a snowflake, the colors forming a glittering pattern. He could see it drifting from the sky, a winter gift from Mother Earth.

"Your work is beautiful, Elaina."

She glanced up and smiled. "Thank you. That means a lot coming from you."

They were looking at each other again, two people who had become husband and wife. "You still haven't told me about your family." He paused, studying the change in her expression, the fading smile, the cloudy blue eyes. "Will you tell me now?" he asked, hoping to learn more about the woman he had married.

Elaina knew she shouldn't be nervous, but talking about her family brought back all those troubled childhood emotions. The anxiety that came with never being quite good enough. The loss of breath. The accelerated heartbeat. The sensation of being trapped with nowhere to go.

She hadn't told Grant about her panic attacks, yet now she was going to tell Nick. She was going to admit out loud what she'd never revealed to another living soul.

"My father died when I was a toddler," she said. "My parents had already been divorced by then. I don't remember him, but I was told he had some Gypsy blood. So whenever I didn't behave according to my mother's satisfaction, she'd say it was the Gypsy in me, the part that lacked grace and breeding."

Nick raised an eyebrow. "I take it she's a critical woman. Impossible to please."

Edging the rosette, Elaina kept her hands busy. "Yes. Wealth and high society are very important to her. She's been married quite a few times, and always to men who improved her social status."

"Is she still with the same man? I remember him from your wedding. And from Grant's funeral, too."

Elaina nodded. "Terence Myers. He's been my stepfather since I was in junior high. He and Mother are well suited. Terence is a successful stockbroker. He owned a home in Malibu when she married him. That's where I spent my teenage years." And although Terence hadn't adopted her, she had been enrolled in school under his name. Elaina Fay Myers, stepdaughter of a prestigious man.

Sit up straight, Elaina. And for goodness sake, fix your hair. Don't embarrass me in front of Terence. His children are so well behaved.

"Your mother's name is Kate or Karen—"

"Katherine." Releasing a heavy breath, she threaded another bead. "Whatever I did wasn't quite right. My tennis game, the clothes I wore." She looked up and saw him watching her. "We didn't come from old money. Nor were we Rockefeller rich. But that didn't stop my mother from being invited to all the best parties or from organizing charity events. She and Terence fit into that world. And so did Duncan and Joyce."

Nick frowned. "Who?"

"Duncan and Joyce. They're Terence's children from a previous marriage. They lived with us, too." To keep herself from sounding like a petty little rich girl, she spoke in a calm, quiet tone. "Joyce is a corporate attorney now, and Duncan is a cosmetic surgeon."

"And you're a teacher," Nick offered gently.

"Yes. A third-grade teacher at an inner-city school. My career choice was a disappointment." Nervous, she laughed a little. "The least I could have done was become a university professor."

"Someone has to teach our young," he said. "Someone has to guide them. Your mother should be proud of you."

She meant to respond, but suddenly she couldn't talk. He studied her, his gaze intense. Those eyes, she thought, those magnetic eyes. The electricity between them still frightened her. Their attraction was so powerful. Dangerous in a way she couldn't describe.

"Elaina?"

Her mouth went dry. "Yes?"

"You would fit in anywhere. You have class, but you're not stuffy. That's a quality to be admired."

She traced the rosette, following the circle with her thumb. "Thank you," she managed, her voice a little raspy. She reached for her coffee and sipped the sweetened drink. "But I never felt comfortable at all those social functions I had to attend." Because she had been worried about pleasing her mother, about doing and saying the right thing. "I used to have panic attacks. My hands would shake, and I'd lose my breath. But I never told anyone, and no one ever noticed." The shame and the fear had been hers, and hers alone. "They stopped happening when I moved out of the house, when my life became my own."

Nick touched her knee, connecting with her robe. "Then you did the right thing. You took control."

"Yes." Her robe slipped through his fingers. Skin and silk, she thought. Man and woman.

A moment later he drew back, rising to pick up the belt he'd been lacing. The buckstitch wove in and out of the leather, strong and tight. "So Grant didn't know?"

She shook her head. "I couldn't bear to tell him. He admired my family, and they respected him. He was a young, handsome, successful advertising executive." Smoothing her robe, she touched the spot where Nick's fingers had been. "Marrying Grant was the only thing I've ever done that pleased my mother. And I felt safe when I was with him. He made me feel like I belonged."

"Your mother didn't criticize you in front of him?"

"No. She treated me right."

"And she didn't care that Grant was Indian?"

"She commented on it, of course." Elaina let out the breath she'd been holding. Talking about her family wasn't as difficult as she'd imagined, at least not to Nick. "But Grant wasn't what she considered a political Indian. He didn't wear his hair long or discuss the injustice that had been done to his people. He never mentioned his heritage, not even in the slightest manner, so to her, he seemed white."

"But he wasn't," Nick said. "Somewhere deep in Grant's heart, he was still Comanche."

"I know that now. If it hadn't been important to him,

he wouldn't have asked you to teach Lexie." Or to marry me, she added silently.

Elaina studied her beadwork. The rosette was finished, and she was ready to begin another. "I'm learning about your heritage, too."

"Yes, you are." He grinned boyishly. "You're a good little Comanche bride."

Releasing the embroidery loop, she glanced up and caught the crooked corner of his smile. She knew he was teasing her, but the compliment made her feel good inside—sweet, dreamy and incredibly warm.

The house sparkled with holiday cheer. Red and green candles flickered on tabletops, and strands of pine-scented garland added yet another aroma to the cozy ranch dwelling. There wasn't a corner that didn't twinkle or a window frame that didn't shimmer.

The air smelled of sugar and spice. And everything nice, Nick thought as he entered the kitchen and saw Elaina.

She closed the oven and removed the protective mitts from her hands, placing them beside the stove.

He sat on the edge of the counter, where a few dozen cookies cooled on a sheet of waxed paper. "You've been busy," he said.

She sent him a feminine smile. "'Tis the season."

"Indeed it is." He had been busy, too. Lexie's and Elaina's gifts were wrapped in colorful paper, hidden in the clutter of his workshop. "The house looks great."

"Thanks, but Lexie did most of it. She can't wait to trim the tree."

Which they had all agreed to do together on Christmas Eve. "Where is she?"

"With Starr and her grandparents. They're making one last trip to the mall." Elaina dipped a butter knife into a bowl of white frosting and began icing holiday-shaped cookies. "Do you want to help? You can sprinkle the candy on top."

"Who, me? Do women's work?" He flashed a silly grin. "I don't think so. I'll just hang around and mooch like a macho guy should."

She laughed and shook her head, curls springing around her face. "Macho guys eat sugar cookies?"

"This one does." Her domestic skills pleased him, as did her appearance. She wore an oversize sweatshirt and jeans, her chestnut locks damp and messy. "You look different, Elaina." Wild, he thought, a little untamed. "Must be your hair."

"Oh." She shifted uncomfortably. "I washed it today, but I haven't had the chance to style it. I'm not going to leave it like this."

"Why not?"

"Because it looks awful."

"I think it looks pretty." He imagined twining his fingers around each rebellious curl, tugging the damp mass and kissing her breathless.

She opened a plastic shaker and sprinkled confetti-type candy over a row of frosted cookie bells. "Are you kidding? My mother used to throw fits over my unruly hair. Which, of course, she attributed to the Gypsy in me."

Unable to resist, Nick snagged one of the bells, then licked the icing before he bit into it. "Is that so? Well, I just happen to like blue-eyed women with tender hearts and tousled hair."

Her cheeks flushed. "Is that what I am?"

"Yes, ma'am."

A timer sounded. Elaina turned away, and Nick finished the treat, watching the way she moved. A properly bred lady, he decided, with just enough Gypsy to make a man's blood swim.

A pan of chocolate chip cookies came out of the oven, filling the room with a freshly baked aroma. She set it on the stove. "Nick?"

He brushed crumbs from his lap. "Yes?"

"I've been thinking a lot about what you did." She fumbled with an oven mitt. "It really means a lot to me."

Confused, he met her gaze. "I'm sorry, but I don't understand. What did I do that was so great?"

She lifted the butter knife, stirring the frosting absently. "You know, the celibacy thing."

Embarrassed, he reached for another cookie and broke it in half. "I thought we weren't going to make a big deal out of that."

"But it was a big deal. At the time, you hadn't even talked to me about marriage. Yes, you'd made a promise to Grant, but there was no agreement between us."

"I already told you how many times I wanted to cheat. I'm not a saint, Elaina. I'm a sexual being, and I missed it."

"But you still remained true to your convictions. You respected me enough to do that. And you didn't go to another woman, no matter how much you needed a release."

"I used to think it was cool that the Comanche got to have more than one wife," he said, offering an explanation. "And I kept that in the back of my head when I went from one lover to the next. But after Grant died, my perspective changed. The old way wasn't about having multiple lovers. A warrior honored his women. He provided protection and loyalty."

"And Grant gave that responsibility to you."

"Yes. He did." And now Nick understood why she was thanking him. He had taken on the job he'd feared most—the commitment that came with marriage. "Hey, at least my brother only had one wife. I'm lucky I don't have a bunch of blue-eyed, wild-haired brunettes nagging me."

"I do not nag." Elaina smacked his arm, and they both laughed.

But a second later they stared at each other. One of those haunting gazes that made him want to touch her, kiss her, pull her into his arms and never let go.

"I've been lying to myself all these years," he said.

She blinked. "What do you mean?"

"I pretended that my mom leaving hadn't affected me as much as it did. Think about it. I'm thirty-six years old, and I've never been in a serious relationship. Grant focused on love, but I didn't let anyone get close to me."

She brushed his hand, and Nick flinched and dropped the cookie halves, feeling like an idiot. "I can't believe I just told you that."

"Why? Are you worried that I'm going to get too close?"

"No. But that's because we're not going to fall in love. That's not what this marriage is about."

She nodded, blew a nervous-sounding breath. "We're a safe bet."

"That's right. We are." And because they were both uncomfortable, he cursed himself for bringing it up. "Why don't we change the subject?"

"What do you want to talk about?" she asked, returning quietly to her task.

"I don't know." He watched her frost little Christmas-tree cookies, trimming them with red and gold sprinkles. "How's your new car running?"

"Fine. I really like it."

"Good." Since the lease on her California car would be up next month, she'd decided to lease a vehicle in Oklahoma to replace it. But letting her condo go, he realized, wasn't quite as simple. "Have you called a Realtor yet?"

"No. I'd rather deal with someone in person. Besides,

I have to go back to L.A. after the holidays. I can't put it off for too long."

"What about Lexie and me?" he asked.

"I think it would be better if I took the trip alone."

"No way." Nick shook his head. "You're not packing that entire house by yourself. Lexie and I are going, too." He wasn't about to allow Elaina to face the condo alone, to box up memories that would trigger tears. "We're a family, and we need to stick together," he said, clinging to the vow he'd made to his brother. He glanced at the festive fare, at the garland, the candles, the shiny gold ribbon. And not just during the holidays. A family should support each other all the time.

Nine

"I'll bet we have the prettiest tree in Oklahoma," Lexie said, stepping back to admire their handiwork.

Elaina smiled at her daughter. "It is beautiful." Painted stars, tiny shields, beaded rosettes, leather-wrapped feathers. They'd blended a Native American theme with traditional ornaments and glittering lights. The angel Nick had placed on top wore a halo of gold and wings of silver.

It was Christmas Eve, and they gathered in the living room, dressed in comfy sweats and silky pajamas. Flames danced in the hearth, and a bundle of sage purified the air.

"Can I sleep out here tonight?" Lexie asked.

A lump formed in Elaina's throat. "You used to do that when you were little."

"I know. I remember." The young girl looked at her uncle. "I used to leave cookies for Santa, and then fall asleep on the couch waiting for him to come."

Nick moved to stand beside her. "Did you ever see him?"

"No, but the cookies were always gone. Of course, it was Daddy who ate them. But I didn't know that then."

"They must have been chocolate chip. They were my brother's favorite."

Elaina thought about the variety of cookies she'd baked this year. As always, she'd made two dozen chocolate chip, with extra chips in the batter, just the way Grant had liked them.

"I think we should each open one present tonight," Nick said. "Then Lexie can sleep on the couch and wait for Santa to bring the rest."

"That's so cool. Can I leave cookies?"

He grinned. "Sure."

"Will you eat them?" she asked.

"You bet." He put his arm around her and gave a gentle squeeze. "I like the frosted ones with the sprinkles on top."

The sugar cookies, Elaina thought. Big, strong, tough Nick really did like kid-type treats.

Lexie knelt in front of the tree, looking like a little girl with bright holiday eyes. "Can I open two? One from each of you guys? That way I won't hurt anyone's feelings."

Elaina glanced at Nick, and he grinned back at her. "Are we being conned?" he asked.

"Yes, but she has a point."

Minutes later, Lexie tore into a package from Elaina—a box filled with hair ornaments. She hadn't been able to resist buying her daughter hearts, butterflies and jewels. She'd purchased some at department stores and others at a little antique shop she'd discovered on the outskirts of town.

Lexie examined each barrette with pure feminine delight. "I'm letting my hair grow," she proclaimed, leaning in to embrace her mother.

Because she was maturing, Elaina thought, holding her child close. Blossoming into a delicate young lady.

The next gift was from Nick. Lexie opened it and discovered a leather headstall, decorated with silver bars and engraved conchos.

"It's for the horse I'm going to buy you," he said. "I figured we could look for one after the holidays. You should be involved in choosing your own mount."

A girlish squeal and a sturdy hug followed. Elaina studied her family, thinking how beautiful they were. Firelight bathed them in a gentle glow, warming dark eyes and chiseled features. Lexie resembled her uncle, but Nick and Grant had shared the same genes.

"It's *Ap*'s turn," Lexie said, handing Nick a medium-size box. "This is from Mom and me."

Instantly nervous, Elaina chewed her lip. She and Lexie had labored over a personal gift for Nick. Finally they'd decided to make him a pair of Comanche-style moccasins, sized from a simple, store-bought pair he often wore. With Ryan's help Lexie had cut the pattern and stitched the shoes, and Elaina had decorated them with tiny glass beads. It had been a frantic, emotional project, constructed in the wee hours of cold, misty mornings.

Nick opened the box and lost his breath. "They're incredible. I can't believe you did this. Both of you."

He put the moccasins on, then lifted Lexie with a masculine whoop. He spun her around, and she laughed. When he set the young girl down and reached for Elaina, her heart nearly leapt out of her chest.

He kissed her, a warm, soft press of mouth against mouth. A sensuous shiver slid down her spine. Suddenly she needed him. Tonight. On the eve before Christmas, with the wind blowing and the moon high in the sky.

"Open your gift," he whispered against her lips.

She stepped back and felt her hands tremble. You're my gift, she wanted to say. The protector Grant gave me.

The box was small and carefully wrapped. She tore the paper, and saw that Lexie watched. "I was with *Ap* when he bought it," her daughter said. "It's perfect for you, Mom."

Perfect didn't begin to describe the necklace her husband had chosen. A bright blue gem sparkled in a stunning gold setting. It was neither fancy nor simple. It was, Elaina thought, a unique design representing the name of the men she had married.

"Bluestone," she said, her eyes watering.

Nick slipped the chain around her neck. The stone fell in the center, cool and vibrant against her skin. "For a blue-eyed lady," he said.

A short while later, they tucked Lexie onto the couch, with a plate of cookies on the coffee table beside her. She looked up at Nick. "Don't forget to eat them. You're supposed to be Santa."

"I know, baby. But first you have to fall asleep."

As Lexie snuggled beneath the covers, Elaina reached for Nick's hand, and they walked to their room.

She closed the door and met his searching gaze. "Let's make love," she said. "Now. Tonight."

He stroked her cheek, then stepped back "Are you sure?"

"Yes."

"You won't regret it in the morning?"

"No." She moved toward him, stopping when they were but inches apart, the air between them soft and se-ductive. "You're my friend, Nick. But you're my husband, too. You're here for me whenever I need you." He had treated her with honor and respect. And now she wanted to give him the warmth and intimacy they both craved.

"We're good together," she whispered. The power, the lightning, the beauty that only they could create. "I want to feel you inside me." As deeply as possible, she thought, wondering if they could make rain.

Nick carried her to bed, and they undressed each other, their tongues meeting in a wet kiss.

They took their time, exploring, caressing. He covered Elaina's body with his, and she held him while he nuzzled her neck, buried his face between her breasts and made her sigh.

She still wore the blue stone he'd given her, and his wrists were shackled with the sterling bracelets he never removed. Somehow, the metal against flesh aroused her even more.

As he turned his head and captured an impossibly hard nipple, she encouraged him to suckle.

He smelled of man and mystery, his woodsy scent wrapping itself around her like the night. Moonlight shone through the windows, and Christmas lights twinkled in the distance, shimmering like a holiday rainbow.

She touched him—everywhere. He was solid and real, his breath quickening in raspy pants. Desperate, anxious, she rolled until she straddled him.

He smiled and drew an imaginary line from her heart to her navel. She obliged, tracing the tattoo on his stomach, the mark that was uniquely his. The Comanche Thunderbird was hovering in the sky, she thought, waiting to unleash Nick's power.

He fisted a condom and handed it to her and, for a moment, it seemed as though he had produced the colorful packet from thin air.

"You're magic," she said.

"So are you."

He reared up to kiss her, and she tore into the foil and rolled the latex over him, stunned by the rhythm of her heart, the pounding of anticipation.

Her nails bit into his back; his fingers clamped her waist. Elaina impaled herself, and Nick drove into her at the same time.

She rode him breathlessly, arched like a bow, her muscles taut. She moved with desperation, with blinding heat. She wanted to reach that glorifying peak, climb the nearest mountain and come tumbling helplessly down.

And when it happened, when lightning flashed from Nick's soul to hers, she heard the patter of rain falling from the sky.

The days after Christmas were quiet. Nick spent lazy afternoons in front of the TV, and Elaina shopped, determined, it seemed, to take advantage of every postholiday sale.

She had been adding feminine touches to their home—leafy plants, little baskets of potpourri. She had even purchased a set of silk sheets for the bed, intensifying their lovemaking with a luxurious texture.

Nick lifted a cup of midday coffee and took a sip. He liked being married. He liked the warmth and tenderness Elaina gave him, the sweet smiles and home-cooked meals.

"Is Mom home yet?"

Startled by Lexie's voice, he turned away from the TV and nearly spilled the hot drink. The girl sounded frantic. "No. Why? What's wrong?"

"I need to talk to her. Please. You have to find her."

"Baby, I have no idea where she is. She had a list of errands to run. Can't you talk to me?"

"No." Lexie crossed her arms, hugging herself through shuddering breaths. "It's girl stuff."

Nick came to his feet, but when he reached out to touch her, she took a step back, clearly on the brink of tears.

"Does this have anything to do with Ryan?" Girls cried over boys, didn't they? And Ryan was Lexie's first painful crush.

"No. And don't you dare say anything to him. I'd die if he found out."

Nick had no idea what humiliating secret he wasn't allowed to reveal to Ryan. Lexie wasn't making a bit of sense. "Please, tell me what's going on. I can't help if you don't tell me."

"There's nothing you can do." She glanced away, avoiding eye contact. "You're a guy."

"I'm not just any guy. I'm your *ap*." The clueless man who felt like a big, useless oaf. What could possibly be wrong? he wondered. What kind of "girl stuff" would a twelve-year-old refuse to tell a man?

Something embarrassing. Something—

When the answer hit him, he staggered, gulping the air that escaped his lungs.

Lexie had just started her first menstrual cycle. That had to be it. The reason she wouldn't meet his gaze, the reason she needed her mother.

Nervous, Nick glanced at his watch. Elaina probably wouldn't be home for hours. "Okay...I-I...um," he stammered, searching for the appropriate words. "I think I know what's going on."

Lexie didn't look at him. She just stood with her arms wrapped around her middle.

"Did you call Starr?" he asked, struggling to get through this. "I'm sure her mother or grandmother would be glad to help."

"They went out of town. They won't be back until tomorrow."

"Oh, yeah. I forgot." He pulled a hand through his hair, wishing he knew what to say or do. This was an important time in a Comanche's girl's life, but it wasn't a man's place to speak of such things. In the old days a menstruating female, whether she was married or single, had the capability of nullifying a man's power.

But this wasn't the old days. And Lexie stood before him, shy and teary eyed.

"Do you need anything?" he asked. "You know, from the drugstore?"

She shook her head, her cheeks coloring to a rosy hue. "I know where Mom keeps that stuff."

"Okay. Good."

Silence stretched between them, and Nick realized he was completely out of his element. He couldn't broach a subject that would make Lexie even more uncomfortable than she already was. She needed a woman to talk to, someone who understood how she felt.

"How about if I call Vera?" he said finally. He moved forward, wishing he could hold his niece, give her the comfort she needed. "She can answer any questions you have. And she can explain the Comanche way. She can teach you what this means in our culture."

Lexie shifted her gaze, glancing at him for a second, her voice broken. "I hope she's home."

"Me, too, baby." He picked up the cordless phone and dialed the number. "Me, too."

Nick waited for Elaina in their bedroom. She was with Lexie, having what he assumed was a mother-daughter talk.

He rolled his shoulders and discarded the novel he couldn't concentrate on. Today had been a frightening introduction to fatherhood. He hadn't been prepared for something like this.

The door opened, and he looked up.

"Hi," Elaina said. She came toward him and sat on the edge of the bed. "How are you holding up?"

"Fine. How's Lexie?"

"Actually, she's doing well. Nick, I appreciate what you did. Vera really helped." Elaina removed her shoes and socks and curled up next to him. "Even though

Lexie knew what to expect, she was still nervous. It's a confusing time in a young girl's life."

"As long as she's okay." He adjusted the quilt, covering Elaina's feet. The room was a little cold, the air outside brisk and windy. "Do you think she'll ever look me in the eye again?"

She rested her hand on his knee. "Yes, but not this week. She's taking the early taboos quite seriously. At least this first time."

He nodded. He knew what Elaina referred to. A Comanche girl took precautions during her cycle. She didn't prepare a man's food or touch his belongings. Nick knew this was Lexie's way of respecting his medicine. It made him proud.

"When it's over, Vera is going to take Lexie to a creek so she can bathe. That's what the women used to do."

He smiled. "A creek, huh? It's going to be cold this time of year."

"I know." Elaina smiled, too. "But Lexie's determined to follow the early practices." She kept her hand on his knee. "By the way, I saw a doctor this morning."

The change in topic startled him. "Why? What's wrong?"

"Nothing. I got on the Pill."

"You didn't have to do that." He was used to keeping condoms available. Safe sex had become habit, something he normally didn't think twice about. "I wouldn't let you down."

"I just wanted to be sure."

"Oh." Nick frowned, wondering why her decision bothered him. She had a right to make choices about her own body.

"It will make spontaneous sex easier," she said.

And conception virtually impossible, he thought. Condoms were a method of birth control, too. But somehow they didn't seem as final as the Pill. Condoms didn't provide long-term protection.

And that was the problem, he realized, the part that bothered him. To Nick, the Pill meant Elaina didn't want to have his children, not even in the future.

He closed his eyes, recalling the first time he'd seen Lexie. He and Grant had stood at the maternity window at the hospital, peering through the glass.

"I'm so glad you're here," Grant said. They were shoulder-to-shoulder, their voices hushed.

"I wouldn't have missed this." Nick had gotten on a plane soon after Grant had called him with the news. "She's your daughter. Alexandra Lee Bluestone." He looked at his twin and saw tears in the other man's eyes.

Grant blinked. "We're going to call her Lexie. Every kid should have a nickname." He placed his hand against the glass. "You know what, bro? I feel like I finally did something important, something that really matters. I helped create a life. A perfect little being."

Nick stared at the baby. She had a cap of black hair, a face like an angel. A puckered angel, he thought with a smile. His niece was the most beautiful little prune ever born.

"Makes you want one, doesn't it?"

"Maybe. Yeah. I suppose it does. But you know it's not going to happen."

Grant slipped a Cuban cigar into Nick's pocket. It was the third one he'd given him that afternoon. "Sure it will. You'll settle down one of these days."

They stood there for another thirty minutes, just watching Grant's daughter.

And now, twelve years later, Nick was wondering how it would feel to have a baby with Elaina.

"Are you all right?" she asked. "You seem troubled."

He opened his eyes. "I'm okay. It's just been an emotional day." And getting more emotional by the minute. He had no right to feel this way. Their union wasn't like other marriages. They'd made a commitment, but it was based on friendship, not love. They weren't planning on having a houseful of babies, children with her sweet smile and his bronze skin. Lexie wasn't destined to have little brothers and sisters giggling at her feet.

Elaina put her head on his shoulder, and he stroked her hair. The chestnut curls rioted around her face in natural disarray, each strand glittering in the amber light.

"You wore it this way for me," he said. "Wild and free."

She nodded. "I'm still trying to get used to it, though."

His heart stirred. A warning, he thought. A prelude

to danger. He couldn't allow himself to fall into a misguided fantasy. He could never take Grant's place, not completely. And to wish for such a thing would dishonor his brother.

"You've made such a difference in my life," she said.

He turned to look at her. "I have?"

"You've made me think about my roots."

He caressed her cheek, the smooth satin skin that fascinated him. "The Gypsy girl."

"Some of my father's ancestors were from Romania. I'd like to find out about them, about their customs."

"Then we should go there. Take a summer trip."

"Really?" Her blue eyes got brighter, the same vibrant color as the necklace she wore. "That sounds so romantic. Misty nights and ancient castles. Flowers blooming on hillsides."

Beautiful women with Gypsy blood, he thought. Ladies with jeweled eyes and glittering hair.

She leaned in to kiss him, and Nick's heart went soft. But once again he heeded the warning, telling himself not to feel too much.

Falling in love wasn't part of the vow.

Ten

Nick stared at his wife. "You did what?"

"I already told you. I agreed to watch Tony Junior this afternoon."

He couldn't believe this was happening. He was trying to get the notion of having a baby out of his head, and she agreed to baby-sit. "Have you seen little Tony in action? That kid is the Comanche equivalent of Dennis the Menace."

She rolled her eyes. "He's only a year old."

Nick plopped down on the couch. Maybe this was just what he needed. Having a kid like Tony Jr. around for a few hours ought to cure his fatherly pangs. He adored his friend's son, but, truth be told, the little guy was a holy terror. A bright-eyed, bushy-tailed, chubby-cheeked tornado.

He sent Elaina a lopsided grin. "Mind if I stick around and watch the fireworks?"

"Suit yourself. But there aren't going to be any fireworks. Little Tony will behave for me."

"Sure he will. He'll take one look at you and think, 'This lady's a teacher. I better be good.'"

"Very funny." She began clearing the end tables, placing breakables on higher ground.

While she kid-proofed the place, Nick watched her, thinking how sexy she looked. Her hair, wild and free, spilled over her shoulders in a riot of Gypsy waves. She wore slim-fitting jeans and a silk T-shirt. Elaina favored soft, feminine fabrics—silks and satins and things that clung to her skin.

She studied a set of decorative steer horns on the coffee table, and Nick chuckled. Yep. Tony Jr. could certainly do some damage with those. Most of Nick's cowboy artifacts appeared to be a problem. Horns, antlers and spurs weren't the safest objects to have around a curious toddler.

Fifteen minutes later, Elaina answered the door. Vera entered the house, balancing her great-grandson on her hip. Little Tony's eyes shone bright and alert. He took in the room, wondering, no doubt, what he could attack first. Already he was squirming to get out of Vera's arms.

"I really appreciate this," Vera said. "I have so many errands to run today."

And she would get them done a lot sooner, Nick thought, if she didn't have to chase after Tony Jr. in the bank or the post office. The tyke could make mischief wherever he went.

Elaina took the boy, and Nick popped up to help Vera unload her car. The older woman routinely baby-sat Tony Jr. while his parents worked, so she had access to every toddler essential known to man. And she'd brought half of them with her today. Nick hauled in a high chair, a playpen and two diaper bags stuffed to the gills.

Within no time, Vera was gone. Elaina set Tony Jr. on the floor, and he squealed with delight, clearly assessing his surroundings. Dressed in a colorful playsuit, he stood on sturdy legs, tiny bells attached to a pair of high-top tennis shoes. His flyaway hair was a dark shade of brown, his skin the color of cream-filled coffee. After gazing at everything, he made a beeline for a brass lamp. The bells jingled as he ran.

"No! No!" Elaina tore off after him.

After several bouts of electrical-cord tug-of-war, she made a suggestion. "Maybe we should feed him."

Nick cocked an eyebrow. "We?"

"Come on," she said, removing the cord from the youngster's mouth. "I could use some help."

While Elaina prepared Tony Jr.'s lunch, Nick snapped the toddler into his high chair. The kid gave him a big, sappy grin, and Nick's heart melted. Instantly those daddy yearnings came back.

Elaina brought the boy's meal to the tray. "Look what I've got for you."

Nick noticed she had provided mostly finger foods, bite-size samples the kid could nibble.

Or destroy. The first thing little Tony did was crumble the crackers and sprinkle them all over the floor.

Elaina glanced at Nick, and they both burst out laughing.

Thoroughly pleased with their reaction, Tony Jr. squealed. And because he enjoyed the attention so much, he decided to make an even bigger mess.

He dumped the entire contents of his plate onto the high chair tray, then poured his juice over it and began squishing the concoction between his fingers. While he worked, he kicked his feet, ringing the bells on his shoes.

It was the sweetest, merriest sound Nick had ever heard. He looked at Elaina. She wasn't laughing anymore. Instead she watched Tony Jr. with a gentle expression.

Nick couldn't help himself. He leaned over and kissed his wife.

Their lips met in the briefest whisper, the softest touch. She opened her mouth, and he stroked her tongue. They could have been drifting on a sea of sunlight, a river of warmth. He felt it bathe his heart in a splash of heat.

They separated, and he touched her cheek. Suddenly the kitchen seemed like the most romantic place on earth, especially when little Tony made a happy sound.

Nick turned toward the boy. The kid's chubby face was covered with his gooey lunch, yet that only intensified the feeling.

I want this, Nick thought as Elaina reached for the child. I want to have a baby with the woman I'm not allowed to love.

Elaina stood in the bathroom doorway, staring at her daughter. It was New Year's Eve, not Halloween, but Lexie wore a faceful of makeup.

Another coat of mascara was being added to the clumps already existing on her lashes. Eye shadow, crooked black liner, a razor-sharp application of blush. She hardly recognized her own child. Not only was she wearing makeup, but her jet-black hair had been teased and sprayed into a little bubble on top of her head.

"What's all this?" Elaina managed.

"I'm getting ready to go out," Lexie said in a matter-of-fact tone. "Starr is having a slumber party. Remember? I told you about it."

"Whose makeup is that?"

"Yours. I didn't think you'd mind."

Elaina took a closer look at the tubes and containers. They were indeed hers. "Lexie, honey, I think you're a bit young for cosmetics."

The girl turned away from the mirror. When she

blinked, her lashes made tiny dots above her eyes. "I'm a woman now."

"You're twelve years old. That hardly constitutes a woman."

With an air of defiance, she added more mascara. "Comanche girls used to get married at sixteen."

"I see." It appeared her child was taking the old ways to an extreme. "And just who do you have in mind for your future husband?"

"Ryan, of course. And Starr said I could have him because she likes Martin Salazar now."

Elaina leaned on the edge of the counter. "Does Ryan have a say-so in this?"

Lexie's shoulders slumped, her womanly confidence fading. "He treats me like a kid, Mom. Like a little sister or something."

And that was the reason she had resorted to eyeliner and a bouffant. "He's four years older than you, honey. At this stage, that's a lifetime. It won't seem that way when you're both adults, but for now, Ryan is treating you the way he should." And he was, Elaina thought, a very honorable young man. He would never hurt Lexie's feelings deliberately. "He's your friend. You should value that."

A pout formed on her shiny lips. "I want him to think I'm pretty."

"You are pretty. Too pretty for all that junk." She studied her daughter's face, the delicate features hiding beneath a pound of goop. "The key to a good makeup job is making it look natural. Let's get one of your fashion magazines, and I'll show you what I mean."

"But I'm already using a picture."

Lexie produced a snapshot resting on the other side of the counter. Elaina gazed at the image. Nick's mother. Her daughter was modeling herself after Pamela Bluestone.

"I realize she's wearing a lot of makeup," Elaina said. "But that was the trend in the sixties. It isn't right for today."

"I like the way she looks."

Elaina sighed. "I know." But the woman in the photograph had hurt her sons. She'd left them feeling confused and abandoned, something Lexie needed to understand. "Pretty people aren't necessarily the most kind. You should admire someone for who they are on the inside, not for the way they look."

The girl frowned. "Are you saying that my grandma was a bad person?"

"No." Once again, the image caught her eye. It was difficult picturing Pamela as a grandmother. "But she did some things that weren't very nice. She left town and never came back to see her sons."

"Am I supposed to hate her?"

"Of course not, but you shouldn't hold her on a pedestal, either."

"Does *Ap* hate her?"

"No. He loved her very much, and I think he still misses her. He was hurt that she didn't come back."

Elaina knew how much Pamela had influenced Nick, particularly his inability to let a woman get too close.

But wasn't he getting close to her? Every moment they spent together became deeper, more emotional.

Maybe, she told herself, as she seized a wave of panic. But they weren't falling in love. That just wasn't possible. Their closeness was based on the need for comfort and companionship. And sex, she admitted, feeling her skin tingle. The nights they spent in each other's arms bordered on obsession, on a physical release both of them craved.

"*Ap* should try to find her," Lexie said.

Confused, she gazed at her daughter. "What?"

"His mom," the girl clarified. "Maybe he should try to find her. Then he won't miss her so much."

Elaina set the photograph aside, wondering if Nick had ever considered looking for his mother. "Maybe," she said, deciding to change the subject. "So, do you want me to help you get ready for the party?"

Lexie nodded.

"Good. Then wash your face and hair, and we'll start over."

"Okay. Are you and *Ap* going out later?"

"Yes." And now Elaina was nervous. Nick wanted to take her dancing, but what if they stumbled all over each other's feet? Or got lost in each other's eyes?

They'd never gone out in the evening before, never faced the outside world as a couple. And tonight they were going to ring in the New Year dancing in a room full of strangers.

This was their first date, she realized, something that seemed softer and sweeter than an arranged marriage.

Elaina and Nick entered a crowded country-and-western club, but what surprised Elaina were the wooden tables and cozy booths. Waitresses rushed by carrying trays laden with charbroiled steaks and barbecued chicken.

She turned to Nick. "I didn't know they served food."

"We're having dinner. Didn't I mention that?"

"Maybe you did." She'd become more and more nervous as the day progressed, and as to whether or not he'd informed her about a dinner reservation, she couldn't be sure.

He studied her expression. "Aren't you hungry?"

She wasn't, but she didn't know how to say no. He had probably gone to great lengths to secure a table on New Year's Eve. The club appeared to be a popular nightspot. Beyond the dining room was a dimly lit bar and a dance floor bustling with activity. She could hear music, as well as the shuffle of a line dance, accompanied by energetic claps and cowboy whoops.

Elaina exhaled a heavy breath, only to find Nick still watching her. "Dinner sounds wonderful." Surely she could summon an appetite. She'd barely eaten all day.

"Great." He approached the hostess, and forty

minutes later they were seated at one of the cozy booths, each with a piping-hot meal in front of them.

They had both dressed for a night on the town. Elaina wore a velvet dress that draped over a pair of suede boots, and Nick had paired a Western shirt with black jeans and a leather jacket. His hair, tousled from the wind, fell onto his forehead, and candlelight shimmered in his eyes. He looked handsome, a little rebellious—a man who had been raised on the fringes of society.

"It's a new year," he said, reaching for his drink. "The start of a new life."

"Yes." Elaina cut into her chicken. She couldn't have predicted this in a million years. Who knew she'd be married to her brother-in-law? Living in Oklahoma? Sharing a bed with him?

"It's strange, isn't it?" he asked, clearly reading her mind.

She nodded, searching for a way to change the subject, to shift the focus without chatting about something as inane as the weather.

"Lexie made a suggestion today," she said, recalling the conversation she'd had with her daughter. "About your mother."

Nick sent her a puzzled look. "She did?"

"Yes. She thought you should look for your mom, find out where she is and what she's doing."

"I've considered it." He cut a portion of his steak into several bite-sizes pieces, then set his utensils down. "But there's a part of me that doesn't want to know.

When I was younger, I made up stories about why she never came back. I convinced myself that it wasn't her fault." He took a swig of beer, replacing the bottle with a soft thud. "She lost her memory. The guy she lived with was holding her captive. I created all kinds of scenarios."

"I'm sorry, Nick."

He shrugged, pulled on the beer again. "It's okay. I'm a big boy now."

But he was still hurting, she thought. Still wishing his mother had cared enough to contact her sons.

"What about you?" he asked. "Have you called your folks yet? They're back from Switzerland, aren't they?"

"Yes, but I haven't had the chance to call." In all honesty, she had been avoiding her parents. She knew her mother would criticize her marriage, insisting it was a foolish, impulsive thing to do.

Nick returned to his steak. "We're leaving for California in a few days. Are you going to call them before we get there?"

"Yes. I don't think surprising them will be a good idea." She couldn't just show up with a new husband in tow. Forewarning them would make things easier.

"They're not going to like me, are they?"

"They've already met you." And her mother hadn't approved of his silver-and-denim style, referring to him as Grant's "hellion" brother. Elaina thought about Nick's tattoo, about the bold design that connected him to the elements. His indigenous spirit made him seem a bit wild, but it made him special, too.

"Yeah, they've met me. But I wasn't your husband then." He frowned, his voice rough. "Let's face it, I'm not Grant. And I never will be."

"You're his twin, not his clone. No one expects you to behave like him." They were distinctly two separate men, yet there were moments she found herself melting in Nick's arms, clinging to the dreaminess he made her feel.

Would it be so wrong to love him? she asked herself. To love the man she had married? The man who was devoted to her daughter?

Yes, a small voice in her said. She couldn't put herself through that kind of pain again. Grant's untimely death had proved that love wasn't worth the risk.

Elaina lifted her wine and took a small sip. Why was she even worrying about this? Nick wasn't looking for an affair of the heart. And neither was she. Friendship was more than enough.

"The music's changed," he said, interrupting her thoughts.

She nodded, realizing he was right. The upbeat tempo was gone, and so were the whoops and howls. A tender ballad drifted from the bandstand.

"Do you want to dance?" he asked.

Elaina accepted his invitation, knowing she would be safe in his arms. They wouldn't trip over each other's feet, and they wouldn't get lost in each other's eyes. It was, after all, only a dance, a pattern of rhythmic movements.

Nick paid their dinner bill and escorted her to the bar, where they waded through a country crowd. A variety of patrons wore party hats, paper crowns and colorful cones, strapped to their Stetsons. Friends and lovers socialized while strangers stood shoulder-to-shoulder, soaking up the festive atmosphere. The band sported fancy Western garb, and bartenders poured champagne.

The music was slow and easy, the dance floor filled with swaying couples. Above their heads, helium balloons hovered like multihued clouds.

Nick escorted Elaina onto the floor, and they claimed a tiny space in the crowd. He slipped his arm around her, and she leaned into him. But when someone bumped her shoulder, she nearly stumbled. She looked up at Nick, and they both laughed. Maybe they would trip over each other's feet.

Or get lost in each other's eyes, she thought as they began to move. Their bodies fit together as one, smooth and fluid, their heartbeats keeping time.

He lowered his head to kiss her, and at that tender moment they could have been the only two people on earth. He tasted warm and exotic, his lips flavored with a hint of beer. Unable to let go, Elaina clung to him, insisting they weren't falling in love.

They felt so good, so right together because they were dancing—gliding to the same flawless rhythm.

* * *

Nick parked his truck in the driveway. He turned to Elaina, thinking how breathtaking she looked. Even in the dark he could see the blue of her eyes, the copper glitter in her hair.

"Did you have a nice time?" he asked.

She smiled. "You know I did."

"Yeah." He grinned back at her. They'd danced the entire night. And not just to slow songs. They'd donned those goofy party hats and joined in on the lively ones, too, laughing and clapping with the rest of the crowd. It had been a perfect New Year's Eve celebration, romantic yet fun.

And now their gazes were locked.

Cueh, he thought, cherishing the woman he'd married. He wanted to give Elaina everything she desired, every hope, every dream, every vibrant moment life had to offer. He longed to make her happy, to see her shine like a bright, spinning penny.

"Oh, my goodness." Suddenly distracted, she broke eye contact, turning toward the windshield.

He shifted, too, then brushed her hand, skimming her fingers with his. A light snow had begun to fall, dusting the hood with a pearly frost. "It's a gift for the New Year." A special gift for the lady with the lapis eyes, he thought. Elaina had been waiting anxiously for this season's first snowfall.

"Let's play in it," she said, sounding like an eager child.

He laughed. "There isn't enough to play in."

"Yes, there is."

She opened the truck door and stepped outside. He followed her, awed by her beauty. She was bundled in a bulky sheepskin coat, lifting her face to the sky. Snowflakes fluttered around her, lighting on moonlit skin and Gypsy hair.

He came toward her, and she reached for him. Standing in the center of the yard, they held each other. By morning a white blanket would cover the ground and mountaintops would shimmer with silvery peaks. But even so, Nick knew the snow would melt much too soon, and he wanted this night, this feeling to last forever.

Greedy, he kissed her, his mouth hungry for hers. She unbuttoned her coat and brought their bodies closer. He could smell her perfume, melding with the brisk winter air, like rose petals drifting over ice.

A new year. A new life. A new sensation.

Sex in the snow.

He guided her to a darkened spot beneath an ancient tree. It was nearly 3:00 a.m., and evergreens flanked this side of the property. He knew they would blend into the shadows, lovers no one could see.

"Tell me you want to," he said.

"I do." Her voice, edged with arousal, brushed his ear. And then her tongue followed, teasing him with feminine foreplay.

He turned his head and captured her lips, tasting

snow and woman, rose petals and heat. Desperate for more, he pushed her against the tree.

And when she removed her panties and slipped them into his pocket as easily as a handkerchief, Nick's blood roared in his head. While he freed himself, she adjusted her hips to accept his penetration, using the rugged bark for support.

He plunged hard and deep, so deep Elaina lost her breath. It escaped into the night, a sigh, a shiver, a streak of lightning that whispered his name.

Her dress bunched at her hips in a crush of black velvet, and a pair of lace-edged hose ended at the tops of her thighs, like smoke sliding over silk. They were fully clothed, making wild, wicked love.

Nick felt the earth shift, the sky open, the world spin with every urgent stroke. She clung to him, gasping with throaty, pleasured pants. He buried his face in her hair, let the riot of snow-dampened waves seduce him.

Pushing deeper still, he moved in mankind's most passionate dance. She was warm and slick, closing around him in an erotic slide of flesh against flesh.

Moonlight slipped through trees, and he saw her eyes flash, blue stones burning into his.

"You're mine," he said. "Tonight you're mine."

Just this once, he thought, he needed to possess her, to brand her, to make her his and his alone. Because no matter how much he denied it, Nick knew what was happening.

He was falling hopelessly, dangerously in love with his brother's wife—a woman he had no right to claim.

She reached for him, drawing him closer, steeping him in need. A blinding, shocking, painful need. Lost in emotion, Nick battled his heart, his mind clawing for control. Elaina's eyes were still flashing blue fire, her gasps still throaty and raw.

And when a climax ripped through her, he felt it rise to the sky, summoning a flurry of wind, a fresh gust of snow.

Desperate to follow, he gripped her hips, and with one last powerful thrust, he convulsed and spilled into her—his body, as well as his soul, crying out for relief.

Eleven

Nick stood before a row of floor-to-ceiling windows, staring out at the city. Glass surrounded the condo, offering multiple views. From his vantage point, California seemed endless, the night sky going on forever. Lights glittered like stars, and a maze of streets led to the fast-paced, trendy world of Westwood. Somewhere out there was UCLA, the university where Grant and Elaina had earned their degrees. Another city block hosted the medical center where Lexie had been born.

Nick's heart constricted. Grant, Elaina and Lexie. They had been a beautiful family, and happiness should have been theirs to keep.

He turned away from the window and studied the condo. Boxes were stacked in corners, knickknacks and collectibles packed carefully. But even in its barren stage, the interior still reflected Grant's contemporary taste. Tables were sharp and angular, the couches upholstered in Italian silk.

Elaina and Lexie slept down the hall, both resting fitfully. Nick had tried to sleep, but he'd gotten out of bed, choosing to roam the house instead, the clock nearing midnight.

Sinking into a leather recliner, he exhaled a ragged breath. "I'm in love with your wife, *bávi*," he whispered to his twin. "But I didn't mean for it to happen."

Nor had he meant to put Grant in danger. But he'd done that, too.

Nick closed his eyes, and memories flooded his mind, like the edges of a misty dream, pulling him back in time, back to the night his brother had died.

The sports bar had been cramped and noisy, and they'd been ribbing each other all night, laughing and joking like a couple of kids.

They both knew they stood out in a crowd, but identical twins often did. Even with the difference in their hairstyles and the type of clothing they wore, their resemblance was unmistakable. Two men with the same towering height and muscular build were hard to miss, especially if their faces bore the same strong-boned features.

The cocktail waitress approached, her tray filled with empty bottles. "Can I get you guys another beer?"

Nick leaned against the pool table. He'd just lost three games in a row. "No, thanks. I'm fine."

"Me, too," his twin added, twisting what had to be a lucky cue. "We're about ready to go."

The waitress moved on, and Nick studied Grant's cocky grin. "Any chance you'll let me drive that machine of yours anyway?" he asked, referring to the wager they'd placed on Grant's new car.

"Hell, no, country boy. I kicked your butt fair and square."

The older twin was still grinning as they walked out to the parking lot. He bumped Nick's shoulder, and they both laughed. Grant's shiny black turbo-charged toy didn't really interest Nick. He was a four-wheel-drive kind of guy, and they both knew it.

Grant pressed a button on his key chain and turned off the alarm. He slid behind the wheel while Nick climbed into the passenger's seat.

They headed down a major street, hitting every red light imaginable. The Carrera purred in neutral, waiting, it seemed, to arch its sleek European body and devour the concrete jungle.

And there was plenty to devour. The freeway was a long, dark stretch of nearly empty lanes. But 1:00 a.m. wasn't the height of traffic hour.

"Are you sure you can't stay for a few more days?" Grant asked. "It seems like you just got here."

"I know, but I can't spare any more time away from

work. I've got too many orders to fill. I have to catch that plane tomorrow."

"I'll miss you."

"Yeah, me, too." Nick glanced at his twin, grateful he'd been given a brother, someone who loved him without reserve. They weren't ashamed of the affection they felt for each other, and they'd never tried to act macho and hide it. More than likely, they would both get sappy-eyed at the airport.

They rode in silence for a while, but as a vehicle several car lengths ahead swerved and skidded to the side of the road, they both let out quick, jerky breaths.

"Damn, that scared me." Grant cut his speed as they neared the stranded Mercedes, which had come to an uneven stop.

Nick looked out the window and saw three young men exiting the vehicle. "Some guys just got out. I think they're teenagers."

"Really? In a car like that?" Grant patted himself down. "Doesn't it figure? I forgot my cell." After passing the Mercedes, he checked his rearview mirror. "I guess it doesn't matter. They seem to be all right."

Nick continued to glance back. "You mean we're just going to leave them there?"

"They didn't crash, bro."

"But it's the middle of the night."

"And this is L.A. Unless somebody's bleeding, we drive on by."

"I can't believe you said that." Nick stared into the darkness. "They're kids."

"Yeah." Grant shot him a cynical look. "And that's exactly my point. What if they're drunk or stoned? Or out joyriding in a stolen car?"

"Boy, the big city has really done a number on you. You know damn well their tire blew. That can happen to anyone. And they're probably driving their parents' car." Parents who would worry, he thought, if their children didn't come home on time. "You're condemning them for being young."

Grant sighed in exasperation. He exited the freeway and reentered on another on-ramp, doubling back.

And when he pulled in behind the Mercedes, he dropped the attitude and grinned at Nick. "Satisfied, little brother?"

"Yeah. But I'm your younger brother. Not your little one."

They both laughed and got out of the car. Grant had beaten Nick into the world by a whole two minutes.

The teenage boys seemed glad to see them. They had a flat, but their jack was broken. Grant offered to let them use his. He went to his car and opened the trunk, and Nick came up beside him.

"See," he whispered. "They're just average kids."

"Okay. So I overreacted."

Clutching the jack, Grant faced the teenagers. And the instant Nick turned around, one of the average-looking kids fired a gun point-blank into his brother's chest.

Nick's knees buckled as Grant fell. The jack hit the ground with a resounding clank, and the youth aimed the gun at Nick, but the bullet never connected.

"Shoot him!" someone shouted.

"It's jammed," came the frantic reply.

"Then leave him. Let's just go. We've got to get out of here."

In the chaos and the fear, Nick cradled his twin. Grant's shirt was sticky with blood, his breathing slow and labored. The Porsche flew into the night, a murderer behind the wheel.

"Oh, God. Dear God." Nick shrugged out of his jacket and pressed it against Grant's chest, struggling to stem the wound. "I'm so sorry. I did this to you. I did this." He knew his brother was dying. He could feel Grant's heartbeat fading. The other heartbeat, the one he'd slept beside in the womb.

"Not your fault…Nicky…not…your fault."

Tears sprang to his eyes. "I love you, *bávi*." My older brother. My other soul. What am I going to do without you?

"Love you, too…*rámi*." The last word was a soft, almost silent whisper, but the impact was strong. *Rámi.* Younger brother. For the first time in years, Grant had spoken the language of their ancestors.

They gazed at each other, and in the dark of night

Grant asked Nick to take his place, to teach his daughter and protect his wife.

And the moment the vow was made, the moon floated gently across the sky, and Grant Bluestone, the older brother, the other heartbeat, died.

"Ap? Are you all right?"

Nick looked up to see Lexie coming toward him. He still sat in the living room, surrounded by city lights. "I'm fine," he said, letting out the breath he'd been holding. He could still hear the gunshot, the metallic blast echoing in his mind. "I just had a little trouble sleeping. What are you doing up, baby?"

"I was thirsty."

He noticed the empty glass in her hand. "Do you want me to tuck you back in?"

"Okay."

She set the glass on the coffee table, and they walked quietly to her room. When she crawled into bed, he kissed her forehead.

She closed her eyes, and he secured the blanket around her. "Snug as a bug."

Her eyes came open. "Daddy used to say that."

"I know."

They smiled at each other, and Nick thanked his twin with a silent prayer. Grant hadn't blamed him for what had happened that night. Instead he'd entrusted Nick with his wife and child, with a beautiful, ready-made family.

Because my brother loved me, he thought. And love meant healing. And forgiveness.

He left Lexie's door open and entered the master bedroom. A low light burned, casting misty shadows on pale beige walls. Trapped in a fitful sleep, Elaina tossed and turned.

Her Gypsy hair was strewn across a pillow, and a silky nightgown was tangled around her legs. Sometime during the evening she had kicked away the covers, leaving herself vulnerable to the night.

He sat on the edge of the bed and drew the blanket around her. I love you, he wanted to say. You're my wife, and I love you.

"Nick?" Her eyes, edged with lavender circles, fluttered, then opened. "Where have you been?"

"I was in the living room, and then I put Lexie back to bed. She got up to get a drink of water." Somehow, it didn't surprise him that Elaina sensed he had been gone. They were both light sleepers, aware of each other at every restless moment. He climbed into bed beside her, and she snuggled against him.

He couldn't tell her what was on his mind. Not here. Not now. He would wait until they were back in Oklahoma, until the stress and sadness became more bearable. Packing the condo wasn't easy. For Elaina, it held over a decade of bittersweet memories.

"I'm nervous about tomorrow," she said.

He stroked her hair, slipping his fingers through the

tousled waves. "About going to your parents' house? Don't worry. Lexie and I will be there, too."

"I know. But my mother wasn't very nice on the phone. She said our marriage was destined to fail."

"Then we'll prove her wrong. We did the right thing. We did what Grant asked us to do."

And in the process, Nick had fallen in love. He could only pray that Elaina would understand when he told her how he felt. Because if she returned his love, he could learn to be whole again.

But if she didn't, he thought, fear creeping in, what was left of his haunted soul might not survive.

A gentle wind blew, and waves foamed as they rolled upon the shore. Seagulls dipped into the swell, the ocean their sanctuary.

Elaina sat on the deck of her parents' private beach-front home, sipping mocha-flavored coffee. Lexie and Nick walked along the shore. Nick's jeans were rolled to his ankles, and Lexie wore a pair of denim shorts. The January weather was pleasant, but not hot enough for swimsuits.

"You're staying for dinner, aren't you? Terence is leaving the office early. He's anxious to see Lexie."

Elaina turned to the sound of her mother's voice. Katherine Myers sat across from her, slim and stately. Ash-brown hair framed her face in an elegant sweep, with golden highlights softening stern, regal features.

"Yes, of course." She couldn't very well deny her step-father the opportunity to visit with his granddaughter.

"Good. I have a wonderful menu planned."

Dinner at the Myers home was never a simple affair, Elaina thought, not even on a casual, breezy day. A private chef, someone her mother had lured away from a local restaurant, always prepared each selective entrée.

"We'll dine on the patio."

Elaina nodded, hiding an amused smile. Her mother wouldn't dream of seating them at a formal table, not when their attire spoke of sand-encrusted denim.

Katherine reached for her coffee. "Lexie seems happy."

Elaina watched her daughter stroll along the shore. The young girl looked lean and graceful, like a filly just coming into her own. "She is. Very happy."

"I'm glad. Terence and I have been worried about her."

"Me, too. But she's doing well. She's looking forward to starting a new school."

Katherine made an unladylike snort. "In Oklahoma of all places."

"Lawton isn't exactly the boonies, Mother."

"Isn't it? My goodness, you're living on Indian land."

Ah, Elaina thought. The expected criticism. Today she would square her shoulders and challenge it. "Lexie belongs to the Comanche Nation. That land allotment is her legacy."

"I suppose." The other woman sipped delicately. "But I'll never understand it."

"Maybe Lexie can explain it to you. She's been learning about her heritage."

Katherine angled her head. "Yes, well. It's quite obvious she's influenced by her uncle."

"She loves him very much." Nick had given Lexie the opportunity to grow, to expand her wings and explore a side of herself she had never known.

"It would certainly help if you loved him, too."

Elaina's jaw nearly dropped. If a giant serpent had just risen from the sea, she wouldn't have been more surprised. Her mother was encouraging her to love Nick? Grant's "hellion" brother? "That's not possible. Besides, Nick and I are fine with the way things are."

"That sounds very civil of you, but I happen to be an expert on this subject. Loveless marriages do not work. I have three ex-husbands to prove it. And after all these years with Terence, I know the difference."

"So do I. And this time you're wrong. Nick and I will make our marriage work."

She shifted her gaze to the sand, where he gathered seashells with Lexie. His hair blew across his forehead in a mass of blue-black strands, and the T-shirt he wore clung to his chest, stretched by the wind. She could still feel the comfort of his arms, the warmth of his skin as he'd held her last night.

He turned to look her way, and she nearly lost her breath. Across the beach their eyes met.

Beautiful Nick. Her kind and generous husband. She wouldn't let her mother diminish what they shared.

Moments later, Nick and Lexie climbed the deck.

Lexie rattled the shells in her pocket. "Grandma, can I go inside and wash these off, then play video games?"

"Yes, but be sure to dust your shorts first. And take off your shoes. I don't want sand all over the carpet."

"Okay." The young girl began brushing her clothes, and Elaina was reminded of herself at that age. In her family, a beachfront home had its drawbacks. If Lexie had been wearing a swimsuit, she would have been instructed to shower and change in one of the private dressing rooms beside the pool.

"Nick," Katherine said, addressing him in a stiff tone. "Join us, please."

He sat next to Elaina, and her heart made a jittery dive for her throat. What was her mother up to? One minute she was trying to talk Elaina into falling in love, the next she was assessing Nick with cool reserve.

As soon as Lexie entered the house, Katherine looked across the table at her new son-in-law. "You're quite different from your brother."

"Yes, ma'am, I am," Nick responded, exaggerating his Oklahoma twang. Reminding her, he decided, of exactly who he was and where he'd come from.

The older woman tilted her head in a queenly manner. "I hope you don't find my line of questioning offensive, but I'm curious about something."

Elaina's back stiffened, but Nick kept his posture

loose. He suspected Katherine Myers was testing his character, attempting, in a sense, to intimidate him. "Feel free to ask me anything you like."

"Thank you. I will." She pursed her lips and drilled him with a haughty stare. "Did you and Grant ever date the same women?"

Nick heard Elaina's sharp intake of breath. He kept his own breathing even and his expression blank. If Katherine wanted to offend him, she'd certainly done it. But damn if he'd give her the satisfaction of seeing him riled.

"No, we didn't," he said.

"Never?" she pressed.

"No. Never."

"But you both married my daughter."

He wasn't sure what point Katherine was trying to make, so he answered as honestly as he could. "Grant asked me to take care of her."

"So you married her out of duty?"

Nick wanted to reach for Elaina's hand and hold it, but her fingers were curled on her lap. "One brother marrying another brother's widow used to be quite common in our culture."

"Maybe so, but that just doesn't work for me." Katherine glanced at her daughter, then back at Nick. "I already told Elaina, so I may as well tell you. I think your marriage is destined to fail."

Elaina finally interjected. "Mother, please don't do this."

Nick challenged Katherine, defending Elaina, as well as himself. "I realize our situation is unusual, but I assure you, we have a kind and caring relationship."

She challenged him right back, her words stunning him speechless. "That's fine and dandy, but that's not exactly the same as being in love."

Love.

Nick breathed in the salty air. He loved Elaina with every soul-clenching part of his being. She was everything he needed, everything he could possibly want.

Rather than respond to Katherine, he glanced at his wife, but her gaze was fixed on the sea. It was just as well, he thought. This was neither the time nor the place to declare his feelings.

Twelve

Three days later, Nick was in Oklahoma, worrying himself into the ground.

"Got any advice on how to handle this?" he asked Kid. The gelding watched him with a curious expression, but Nick supposed he looked like a madman, dragging his hands through his hair and pacing the barn. "I'm a nervous wreck."

Kid tossed his head and snickered.

Nick sent the horse a level stare. "You think this is funny? Well, I wouldn't laugh if I were you. I know you're in love with her, too."

The gray pinned his ears, clearly denying the charges.

"Chicken," Nick muttered, to himself as much as the horse.

He checked his watch. Elaina was probably nibbling a late-morning snack by now. A bagel with cream cheese, he thought, or maybe one of those frilly little cucumber-and-watercress sandwiches she'd grown fond of as a child.

Turning on his heel, he exited the barn. This was as good a time as any. Lexie was spending the weekend with Starr, so he and Elaina had the house to themselves.

A few minutes later, Nick decided his timing was perfect. Elaina sat at the dining-room table, paging through the newspaper, a half-eaten snack in front of her. He glanced at her plate and smiled. A cucumber-and-watercress sandwich, with a bagel on the side. Apparently she hadn't been able to make up her mind.

"Hi," she said.

"Hi." He sat across from her, thinking how pretty she looked. Her hair had been coiled into a hasty topknot, copper tendrils framing her face.

Still feeling anxious, he scooted down in his chair. He couldn't just blurt the words out. Nick had never told a woman that he loved her. Of course, he'd never been in love before.

"Is something wrong?" she asked.

"No. I just thought we should talk." He wished he had a cup of coffee, something, anything to keep his hands busy. Instead, he drummed his fingers on the tabletop, searching for a way to say what was on his mind. "We never actually discussed what happened at your parents' house. You know, the stuff your mom said about our marriage."

Elaina pushed her plate away. "She had no right to put us on the spot like that. I'm sorry if it made you uncomfortable."

"It was a bit awkward, but I think she meant well."

"Maybe, but she doesn't understand our marriage. And no matter what I said to her, she wouldn't listen."

His heart went still. Very still. "So what exactly did you tell her?"

"That she was wrong. That we don't need to be in love to be happy."

He felt his breath hitch, his hands tremble. "So you don't think it could ever happen?" he asked, struggling to keep his pulse steady.

She shook her head. "I won't let it. And neither will you. I like the way things are. Friendship is enough."

Suddenly he couldn't tell her. He couldn't say the words out loud. The hurt was too deep. And so was the guilt. Maybe he had no right to love her, to love his brother's wife as his own.

He came to his feet. And when he stood, he bumped the table. Elaina's plate rattled, then fell, bouncing without breaking. The bagel rolled under the table, and the sandwich flew open, spilling its contents onto the floor.

"Grant died because of me," he said, unable to hide the truth any longer.

"What do you mean? What are you talking about?"

"It was my fault," he explained, wishing that first shot had been fired at him, that he had been the one bleeding on the side of the road. "I convinced Grant to stop for those boys. I insisted on it."

She rose from her chair. "You couldn't have known what they were going to do."

"No, but Grant sensed something was wrong. 'What if they're drunk or stoned? Or out joyriding in a stolen car?' That's what he said. And that was what those kids had been doing. Stealing cars at gunpoint." Nick backed away, knocking his shoulder against the wall. He'd given them his twin. He'd let them take the other heartbeat.

Tears gathered in Elaina's eyes. "I sensed trouble that night, too. I woke up knowing Grant was in danger. It was such an awful, sickening feeling. I called his cell phone, but it rang in the next room."

Nick pictured her, awake and afraid, calling a useless phone. "I'm sorry." He glanced at the floor, then looked up to see her watching him. "So sorry I took your husband away." He stood like a statue, as motionless as a block of carved stone. "Do you hate me?"

"Oh, Nick. It wasn't your fault. You're a kind and decent man. You convinced Grant to stop because you thought those boys needed help."

"They killed my brother."

"And they killed you, too," she said softly. "A part of you died with your twin." She reached out and took his hand, holding it lightly in hers. "I could never hate you."

But she would never love him, he thought. She would never feel for him what she had felt for Grant.

She gazed at him through a mist of tears, and his heart shattered. He glanced out the window. The day was dark and gray. Gloomy, he thought. Like death.

"Are you all right?" she asked. "You look so sad."

"I'll be okay," he said, catching his breath. "For over two years I've been praying for your forgiveness. And now you've given it to me. That's enough, *cueh.* That's all I need."

Yet it wasn't. He needed her to love him, but Elaina thought of him only as a friend. Nick stared at their joined hands, aching from her touch. Somehow he had to find a way to deal with this, to accept his fate.

He tugged his hand back. "I think I should go away for a few days."

"Where will you go?"

"To the cabin."

She searched his gaze. "I don't understand. Are you mad at me, Nick? Did I say something to hurt you?"

He shook his head. It was what she didn't say that hurt. "I just need a little time alone." Time, he thought, to grieve for what could never be.

Elaina sat on the edge of the couch. Nick had left hours ago. And she still didn't understand why he'd felt compelled to go.

None of it made sense. At first he wanted to talk

about what her mother had said to them, and then he'd blamed himself for Grant's death.

Nick's emotions seemed jumbled. And now Elaina's were, too.

She looked out the window. It was still daylight, but the sky was dark, a gunmetal shade of gray. Hugging herself, she closed her eyes. She felt so alone, so confused. Nick was her friend, her husband, her lover, yet she didn't understand his behavior today.

When she'd told him that Grant's murder wasn't his fault, he'd accepted her heart-filled words. He'd even said that her forgiveness was all he needed. Yet that hadn't eased his mind. He'd left for the cabin, clearly troubled.

Opening her eyes, she glanced at the phone. She lifted the receiver, but the number she dialed stunned her. She was calling her mother, longing for the maternal comfort she'd craved all her life.

Katherine answered on the fourth ring.

"Mom, it's me." *Your confused, worried daughter.* "I think my marriage is in trouble. Nick went away for a few days, but he didn't say why."

After Elaina explained further, the older woman sighed. "You should have listened to my advice."

"Your advice? All you did was criticize."

"Is that what you think? Good grief, Elaina. I was trying to make you wake up and smell the roses. You're in love with him. But you're too stubborn to admit it."

Her heart rammed her chest. "That isn't true." It

couldn't be. She wasn't capable of falling in love again. "What you said made me uncomfortable. It was awkward. It was awful."

"Because you're afraid of it."

"Of course I'm afraid of it. My first husband was killed. I've spent years mourning him. I couldn't bear to go through that again."

"Listen to yourself. You won't admit that you love Nick, because you're afraid he's going to die. Well, my goodness, we're all going to die someday."

Tears burned Elaina's eyes. "You don't know what it's like. Daddy died after you were already divorced. You've never been a widow."

"You're not a widow anymore, either," Katherine countered. "Grant's twin brother was willing to marry you. You have a husband now."

She glanced out the window. The sky was still gray, still dark and foreboding. And as her hands began to tremble, she knew.

She loved him. Her knight-in-denim-armor. The man who had pledged his life to her. Somehow he had become her world, a desperate force she could no longer deny.

When had it happened? she asked herself. When had she begun to fall in love? On their wedding night? The moment Nick had held her next to his beating heart?

Or had it been on Christmas Eve, when she'd realized that he was her gift, the beauty in her life, the passion and joy she needed?

Battling her emotions, the shock and the reality of her situation, she adjusted the phone. "Why do you think Nick went away, Mom?"

"I don't know, but I saw the way he looked at you. It's quite possible he's been fighting his feelings, too."

Elaina drew a breath. If Nick thought he was in love, that would frighten him, wouldn't it? He had been a bachelor most of his life, a man who wouldn't let a woman get too close. "I wish I could go to him, but I don't want to invade his privacy. He said he needed some time alone."

"Then stay put," her mother suggested. "One more day won't make a difference."

Yes, she thought. What could possibly happen in one day? She was home, and Nick was at the cabin. They were both caught in a whirlwind of emotion, but at least they were safe.

The path Nick walked narrowed, rock formations jutting on one side, a dappled canyon below. Patches of snow melted along the trail, making the ground damp and slippery.

It wasn't a good day for a hike, but he didn't know what else to do. He'd tried holing up in the cabin, but that hadn't worked. So he'd set out on foot, and now he was doing his damnedest to connect with Mother Earth.

But the connection was bleak.

Elaina didn't love him, and she never would. Friendship was all she could give him.

He wished it hadn't happened, that he hadn't allowed his heart to stumble for hers.

Irony struck him, along with another dose of loneliness. Nick Bluestone had fallen desperately, madly, painfully in love—the man who had learned to keep his emotions in check, the man who had refused to let his lovers get too close.

Weary, he stopped to glance at the sky. Clouds moved across the surface, like smoke from a fire. The world erupted in a gray fog, and he drifted on the edge of it, floating into the deep, dark place where heartache was born. Heartache that was as real as death, as tangible as the blood that flowed through his veins.

It should have been me, he thought. If a twin had to die, then the Creator should have taken the one who had no family. No wife, no child, no one to call his own.

A stone rolled beneath his foot. A reminder that life continued whether you wanted to be part of it or not.

He watched the stone tumble and disappear into the canyon below. And as he scanned the treetops and the treacherous cliffs, the unthinkable happened. Nick realized he was lost. Not just on the inside, but confused about the path he traveled. Suddenly nothing seemed familiar. Dusk neared, but he wasn't sure if he was heading toward the cabin or farther away from it.

This was impossible. His internal compass had never failed him before. And damn it, he knew this mountain range as well as he knew the back of his hand.

To prove his point, he stared at his hand. And when

a shiver knifed his spine, his breath rushed out. His hand trembled. It actually trembled.

Rather than succumb to panic, Nick closed his eyes and listened to the wind. When he heard the faint sound of water, he smiled. A river flowing in the distance, he thought, chips of ice thawing in it.

Instantly he knew where he was. Close enough to get back to the cabin before nightfall.

Relieved, he opened his eyes and continued in the direction he'd originally chosen. And then he wondered why it mattered.

He was still alone and aching to be loved.

Nick took another step, but the snow-speckled trail seemed to shift, the ground frozen in too many spots. His feet slipped out from under him. And within the flash of a heartbeat, he knew it was too late. He was falling, soaring over the ledge like a hawk with no wings.

And when he hit the ground, he felt the shatter of bones and then nothing at all.

Moonlight spilled over the bed in silvery streaks, but Elaina dreamed fitfully. She kicked and flailed, the blankets tangling around her legs like a snake.

He was cold. She could feel the chill, the slice of mountain air. Waves of nausea swept through him. He was conscious, and then he wasn't. Blackness came and went and so did a roller coaster of pain.

She tried to touch him, but he was too far away. She

reached again and connected with the dark, silent shiver of fear.

"Nick." She whispered his name and woke up screaming.

Elaina turned on the light and nearly knocked over the lamp. A dream, she realized as the room came into view, a nightmare.

Releasing the breath in her lungs, she slipped on her robe, closing it with trembling fingers. She fumbled with the belt and glanced at the empty space beside her.

Nick was in the mountains.

In the cabin, she told herself, safe and warm. This wasn't like the night Grant had died. She hadn't been dreaming then.

Because her heart wouldn't quit racing, she flipped through the Rolodex and found the number to the cabin. It was 4:00 a.m., but she couldn't shake the need to hear his voice.

The phone rang and rang. She waited nervously, catching her harried reflection in the mirror, the haunted look in her eyes. Answer, please answer.

She hung up and tried again, punching the numbers carefully. Nick was a light sleeper. He wouldn't doze through a shrieking telephone.

Again, there was no answer. No groggy voice, no familiar hello.

He could be in the shower, standing beneath a pounding spray of water. Nick often showered at odd hours. Insomniacs did all sorts of restless things.

Then why was he was so cold? And why was he slipping in and out of consciousness?

Because something was wrong, dreadfully wrong.

Tears flooded her eyes, clouding her vision as she flipped through the Rolodex again and dialed Tony Horn's number.

"I need your help," she said the moment Nick's boyhood friend answered.

"What? Who is this?"

"It's Elaina. Oh, Tony. Nick is in the mountains, but I think he's hurt." She gripped the receiver, her voice vibrating. She was losing another husband, another man she loved.

Nick opened his eyes, but saw nothing but the pitch of night—trees looming and mountaintops swaying, just waiting to crumble.

The earth moved with every roll of nausea.

"Bávi?" He spoke to his brother, his lips parched, the metallic taste of blood in his mouth.

"I'm here," a voice answered, so softly it could have been the wind.

"Can I come with you?"

"No, rámi. No."

"But I'm so cold."

Nick thought he felt someone holding him, cradling his body, making him warm, but he couldn't be sure. The world had gone black once again.

* * *

Elaina sat beside Tony in his SUV, heading for the cabin. She gazed out the window. The sky blazed in a crush of predawn velvet, streams of lavender peeking through shades of blue.

She checked her watch, hoping the sun would appear soon.

"What did you tell your daughter?" Tony asked.

"Nothing. She's staying with a friend this weekend." Lexie didn't know about any of this, and Elaina couldn't bear to worry her.

"That's good." Tony fiddled with the heater. "Nick is probably ignoring the phone on purpose. People do that when they're upset." Warm air blasted through the vents. "I'm not trying to be nosy here, but it's obvious you two had an argument. Otherwise, Nick wouldn't have taken off."

"We didn't argue. That's not why he left." Her voice quavered, her eyes stinging with the threat of tears. "I think he needed to hear that I loved him." He needed to know that he wasn't the only one falling in love. But Elaina had been too afraid to feel it, to admit it to herself.

And now, God help her, it might be too late.

"You can tell him when we see him," Tony said, sending her a reassuring smile. "But first I'm going to kick his butt for not answering the phone."

Elaina swallowed around the lump in her throat. She knew Tony was trying to make her feel better, but she couldn't shake the fear, the panic vibrating with each breath. Nick wasn't brooding by the phone. He was alone somewhere, broken and bleeding.

The sun rose, a bright orange ball sending streaks of fire across the sky. Elaina prayed it would keep Nick warm until someone found him.

"How do you say husband in your language?" she asked, turning to look at Tony. "How would a Comanche woman refer to the man she married?"

"*Cumahpue.*"

She listened to the pronunciation, keeping the word close to her heart.

The cabin came into view a moment later, a rustic structure flanked by snowcapped peaks. Tony jammed the gearshift into Park. Nick's truck sat a few feet away.

Elaina rushed up the wooden steps, Tony on her heels. He unlocked the door with a key Nick had given him ages ago and charged through the cabin.

Nick wasn't there. His overnight bag was on the dresser, and the bed was made. There weren't any dishes in the sink, nor was there a leftover pot of coffee, on the counter.

Tony called the ranger's office. "I told them how worried we are," he said, relaying the conversation.

Elaina crossed her arms, hugging herself from the chill. She stood on the front porch, aching for her husband. "Are they going to search?"

"They're going to make some inquiries. Check the campgrounds. Find out if anyone has seen him. They're taking this seriously."

"We have to look, too."

"Where?" Tony made a wide gesture. "Where on earth do we start?"

"The canyons. The valleys. Lower ground." If Nick was broken and bleeding, then he must have fallen. "Instinct is all I have." And the connection from her dream, she thought. The ribbon from his heart to hers.

The sun hurt Nick's eyes. He squinted into it, looking for his brother.

"Bávi?"

He waited for a response, but heard nothing.

"Where did you go, *bávi?* Where are you?"

Closing his eyes, he shut out the light.

He would find his brother. Somewhere in the darkness, he would find the other heartbeat.

Frightened, Elaina leaned against a tree. She and Tony had been searching for nearly two hours, combing the canyons and the valleys, the areas closest to the cabin.

"What if no one finds him in time? How many days can he survive out here?"

"Don't say that." Tony scrubbed his hand across his jaw. "Don't even think it."

"But he's hurt." And sun wasn't keeping him warm, she thought. "I can feel the chill. He's so cold."

Tony glanced at his car, his voice a deep quaver. "We can drive a little farther out. Look somewhere else."

Elaina stared into a maze of trees. "What's beyond the forest?"

"I don't know."

She closed her eyes and tried to picture Nick, and when she opened her eyes, she saw a shadow moving behind a tree.

A tall, dark image. A man, a cloud of mist, she couldn't be sure. The forest was dense, branches joining limb to limb, clawing their way to the sky.

It moved again, a hazy figure, slipping through the woods. Broad like a man, willowy like a ghost. Elaina's heart pounded. "Do you see it?"

"What?" Tony gave her a confused stare.

She took off running, chasing the figure, afraid it would disappear.

Tony screamed her name, but she ignored the call. She kept running, over twigs and crumpled leaves, around tall, barren trees. The figure was gray, like a rain-shrouded mist, and then it was gold like the sun. She blinked and saw spots in front of her eyes.

She was losing her mind, chasing shadows, racing after something that wasn't real.

A branch scratched her arm. She stumbled and fell. The dirt was moist, snow melting off the trees. She rubbed her hands on her jeans and kept moving. The shadow zigzagged—floating, it appeared, above the ground. Darting in and out of narrow spaces.

She heard Tony behind her, struggling to keep up, following a woman who had gone mad.

"Elaina!"

She couldn't respond. Her breath was lodged in her throat, but if she took the time to find her voice, she would lose sight of the mist.

It was gray again. One minute it took the shape of a man, and the next it seemed like a figment of her imagination. It shifted, changing with the wind.

Tears burned her eyes. Tony didn't see it. He continued to scream for her to stop.

And then she did. She stopped, because the forest ended, and the figure was gone.

A canyon as wide as the eye could see stretched before her.

Tony nearly bumped into her. Struggling for balance, he skidded. Elaina grabbed his arm, and they both teetered.

The canyon was hollow, with rugged peaks towering around it. She looked up at the mountains, then at the ground below. "He's here. Nick is here."

Tony squeezed her hand. "Then let's find him."

Elaina ran across the canyon, but this time she knew where she was going. Tony didn't scream for her to stop. He followed her, as sure as she was. They both sensed Nick was near.

"Dear God." She dropped to her knees when they found him. He lay beneath one of the cliffs, as still and pale as death. His left leg was bent at an odd angle, his jeans torn. Blood oozed from gashes, from scrapes and cuts all over his body.

She touched his cheek, felt the chill from his skin.

Tony searched for a pulse with trembling hands, then took a deep breath when he found one. "I have to get help." He placed his coat over Nick. "We can't take the chance of moving him."

She didn't have to tell Tony to hurry. He had a cell phone in his car. She prayed he could reach an emergency number, that a connection could be made.

"Nick?" she whispered. "Can you hear me?"

His eyelids fluttered.

Air rushed out of her lungs. "I love you, *Cumahpue*." My husband, my heart. "I love you."

"Elaina?" His voice was as broken as his body. "Am I dreaming?"

"No. I'm real. Tony went to get help. We're going to get you to a hospital."

He met her gaze, his eyes barely open. "You love me?"

She skimmed his cheek. "Yes. I love you."

He kissed her fingers. His lips were bleeding, but he didn't seem to notice. He was in shock, in pain, yet he clung to her words like a lifeline.

"I thought Grant was here," he said. "But then I couldn't find him. I'm so confused."

Elaina looked toward the forest, toward the place where the mist, the shifting figure, had disappeared. "No," she said as Nick closed his eyes. "You're not confused at all."

* * *

The March air was unseasonably warm, and Elaina thought a more beautiful day didn't exist. Nick stood beside her in the barn, balancing himself on a pair of crutches. He'd suffered a concussion, bruised kidneys and a fractured leg, but her husband was recuperating with no permanent damage from his injuries.

Elaina nibbled her smile. He'd taken to wearing the baggiest jeans he could find and splitting them down one side to accommodate his cast. Nick wouldn't dream of giving up denim, not even for a broken leg.

He moved closer to Kid's stall. "Tell Elaina you love her."

The gelding pinned his ears, and Elaina laughed. "I don't think he's ready for this."

"He's going to have to learn to deal with his emotions sooner or later. No one in this house is allowed to suppress his or her feelings. If you love someone, you've got to say it."

"Okay, then I'll go first." Elaina turned to her husband. He met her gaze, and she smiled. His eyes were dark in the morning light, his skin a rich shade of copper. The cuts and bruises had healed, but she would never forget the fear of facing life without him. She thanked God every day for giving her Nick Bluestone.

"I love you," she said.

He leaned in to kiss her. Their mouths came together gently. She tasted man and mint, the dawn of spring, the flow of happiness.

"I love you, too," he whispered, deepening the kiss.

His tongue touched hers, dived and danced. Her breath caught, her heart pounded. She moved closer and felt him shift to welcome her. It was so easy to love, she thought, to need and be needed.

Aroused, she reached for his zipper.

Eager, he made a rough sound. The cast on his leg wasn't an obstacle. There were ways, she knew, of working around it.

Kid poked his nose over the stall and butted Nick's shoulder. Startled, he lost his balance and bumped into Elaina. They nearly tumbled to the floor, then sputtered into laughter. So much for fooling around in the barn.

Nick regained his footing. "Somebody's jealous."

Elaina eyed the horse. "Maybe somebody needs a time-out."

Kid went to the back of his stall and snorted his disgust. She suppressed a giggle. "He reminds me of some of my former students." The bad boys, she thought, who challenged a teacher in every way. "I can't help but adore him."

Nick shifted his weight. "Do you miss teaching?"

"Yes, but I'm not ready to go back to work yet." After everything that had happened, she couldn't bear to leave Nick and Lexie alone. "I want to stay home with my family for a while. I hope you don't mind."

He reached for her hand. "Of course not. Family means everything, Elaina. I'm glad you feel that way. I want you here."

She squeezed his hand. "You're letting your hair grow, aren't you?" It brushed his collar, as thick and dark as the night.

He nodded. "Grant wouldn't want me to mourn forever."

Elaina's heart warmed. It didn't hurt to think about Grant anymore. She knew Nick's brother was resting in a bright, sunny place, watching over them with tenderness and care. She had made peace with her loss.

She was Nick's wife now. And together they would share everything life had to offer. Every treasured hour, every rainfall, every flower, every whisper in the wind. The future was theirs for the taking.

"What about children?" she asked.

"Children?" Nick's pulse shot to the edge of his skin. "As in brothers and sisters for Lexie?"

"Yes." She watched him, waiting for an answer, a maternal light dancing in her eyes.

He wanted to circle her in his arms and spin until they both saw stars. This was the moment he had been longing for.

"How many?" he asked.

She brushed her body against his. "How many do you want?"

He swallowed. "As many as you're willing to give me." She licked his ear, sent a delicious shiver down his spine. He did his damnedest to stay on his feet. He'd experienced some dizziness from the concussion, some days of disorientation, but it hadn't been anything like this. His head was swimming. With happiness. "Are you seducing me?"

"Yes. But I think we better find a nice, comfortable bed."

He nibbled her jaw, slid his mouth over hers just to savor the taste. "Will fresh straw do?"

She sighed. "Not this time. Kid will be jealous."

"Then I better get him his own mare to play with. You're mine."

They retreated to the house. The windows were open, the curtains billowing. He removed his shirt and watched her undress. The sheets were silky against his back, the sensation smooth and seductive. She lowered his jeans and straddled him.

She teased them both, rubbing flesh against flesh, need against need.

He raised his mouth to hers, and they kissed. And kissed.

He couldn't stop. He wanted this feeling to last forever.

She rode him like a dream, a current—a rush of warm, warm water. They clasped hands and looked directly into each other's eyes, a river flowing around them.

And in that moment, in the heat and the intimacy, he knew he was loved.

Epilogue

Dawn broke in a blaze of color. Shades of mauve and streaks of blue shimmered across a summer sky. Nick sat on the porch, waiting for the moment to arrive. He had been up all night, watching the world shift from dark to light.

Lexie came onto the porch, and he turned to look at her, his heart drumming in his chest.

She didn't speak. She painted a black spot on the front door. In Nick's family, that meant the arrival of a new brave. On the day he and Grant had been born, two black spots had been painted on the door.

He stood and smiled at Lexie. "I have a son."

She nodded, then flew into his arms. They hugged, clinging to each other with tears in their eyes. Elaina had chosen to give birth the old Comanche way, with only women in attendance.

Nick touched Lexie's cheek. At fourteen, she had grown into a remarkable young lady. She was as tall as her peers, with a slim, feminine figure and a braid streaming down the center of her back.

"I'm so proud of you," he said. She had helped bring her brother into the world.

Lexie took his hand. "Come inside, *Ap*."

As they entered the house, Vera Horn came out of the bedroom, a midwife by her side. Nick knew the baby's umbilical cord would be wrapped and hung in a hackberry tree. Vera would do the honor, offering his son a long and fortunate life.

"Congratulations," Vera said, her crinkled eyes beaming.

"Thank you." Nick smiled at the older lady, then turned to the midwife to thank her, as well. She wasn't Comanche. Her nomadic ancestors had migrated from India to Europe in the fifteenth century, giving her a Gypsy lineage, just like Elaina.

"Go on," the midwife said. "Meet your son."

Lexie waited with the other women while Nick's heart made one final leap. The room had been purified with sage, the scent sweet and inviting.

Elaina looked up, and he lost his breath. Her hair was damp with perspiration, her skin a little pale. He couldn't imagine a more beautiful woman.

"Hi," she said, cradling the bundle in her arms.

"Hi." He returned her soft greeting.

They smiled at each other. He couldn't find the words to describe this moment. He climbed into bed, and she handed him the child they had created.

The baby's face was round and dark, his hair the color of night. He peered at Nick with sleepy eyes, his fists curled around the blanket.

"He's perfect."

"Yes," she said. "Daniel Grant Bluestone. Our little miracle."

They both fell silent, happiness swirling through the sage-scented room like a mist. Nick kissed her cheek, and she put her head on his shoulder. He knew she was weary. She had labored long and hard to bring a new life into the world. He loved her more now than ever.

Holding the infant's body next to his, Nick felt the gentle rhythm of a tiny heartbeat.

The other heartbeat, he thought, sending a silent message to Grant. *Bávi,* I have a son. A boy to grow up with the daughter you gave me.

Nick turned to his wife. While she slept, sunlight spilled in through the windows, creating a bright, warm path.

Heaven, he thought, here on earth.

* * * * *

Brad shoved the truck into gear and drove to the bottom of the hill, where the road forked. Turn left, and he'd be home in five minutes. Turn right, and he was headed for Indian Rock.

He had no damn business going to Indian Rock.

He had nothing to say to Meg McKettrick, and if he never set eyes on the woman again, it would be two weeks too soon.

He turned right.

He couldn't have said why.

He just drove straight to the Dixie Dog Drive-In.

Back in the day, he and Meg used to meet at the Dixie Dog, by tacit agreement, when either of them had been away. It had been some kind of universe thing, purely intuitive.

Passing familiar landmarks, Brad told himself he ought to turn around. The old days were gone. Things had ended badly between him and Meg anyhow, and she wasn't going to be at the Dixie Dog.

He kept driving.

He rounded a bend, and there was the Dixie Dog. Its big neon sign, a giant hot dog, was all lit up and going through its corny sequence—first it was covered in red squiggles of light, meant to suggest ketchup, and then yellow, for mustard.

Brad pulled into one of the slots next to a speaker, rolled down the truck window and ordered.

A girl roller-skated out with the order about five minutes later.

When she wheeled up to the driver's window, smiling, her eyes went wide with recognition, and she dropped the tray with a clatter.

Silently Brad swore. Damn if he hadn't forgotten he was a famous country singer.

The girl, a skinny thing wearing too much eye makeup, immediately started to cry. "I'm sorry!" she sobbed, squatting to gather up the mess.

"It's okay," Brad answered quietly, leaning to look down at her, catching a glimpse of her plastic name tag. "It's okay, Mandy. No harm done."

"I'll get you another dog and a shake right away, Mr. O'Ballivan!"

"Mandy?"

She stared up at him pitifully, sniffling. Thanks to the copious tears, most of the goop on her eyes had slid south. "Yes?"

"When you go back inside, could you not mention seeing me?"

"But you're Brad O'Ballivan!"

"Yeah," he answered, suppressing a sigh. "I know."

She rolled a little closer. "You wouldn't happen to have a picture you could autograph for me, would you?"

"Not with me," Brad answered.

"You could sign this napkin, though," Mandy said. "It's only got a little chocolate on the corner."

Brad took the paper napkin and her order pen, and scrawled his name. Handed both items back through the window.

She turned and whizzed back toward the side entrance to the Dixie Dog.

Brad waited, marveling that he hadn't considered incidents like this one before he'd decided to come back home. In retrospect, it seemed shortsighted, to say the least, but the truth was, he'd expected to be—Brad O'Ballivan.

Presently Mandy skated back out again, and this time she managed to hold on to the tray.

"I didn't tell a soul!" she whispered. "But Heather and Darlene *both* asked me why my mascara was all smeared." Efficiently she hooked the tray onto the bottom edge of the window.

Brad extended payment, but Mandy shook her head.

"The boss said it's on the house, since I dumped your first order on the ground."

He smiled. "Okay, then. Thanks."

Mandy retreated, and Brad was just reaching for the food when a bright red Blazer whipped into the space beside his. The driver's door sprang open, crashing into the metal speaker, and somebody got out in a hurry.

Something quickened inside Brad.

And in the next moment Meg McKettrick was standing practically on his running board, her blue eyes blazing.

Brad grinned. "I guess you're not over me after all," he said.

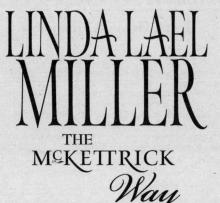

Silhouette®

SPECIAL EDITION™

**brings you a heartwarming
new McKettrick's story from**

NEW YORK TIMES BESTSELLING AUTHOR

LINDA LAEL MILLER

THE McKETTRICK *Way*

Meg McKettrick is surprised to be reunited
with her high school flame, Brad O'Ballivan,
who has returned home to his family's
neighboring ranch. After seeing Meg again,
Brad realizes he still loves her. But the pride
of both manage to interfere with love...until
an unexpected matchmaker gets involved.

—— McKettrick Women ——

Available December wherever you buy books.

REQUEST YOUR FREE BOOKS!

2 FREE NOVELS PLUS 2
FREE GIFTS!

American **R O M A N C E**®

Heart, Home & Happiness!

YES! Please send me 2 FREE Harlequin American Romance® novels and my 2 FREE gifts. After receiving them, if I don't wish to receive any more books, I can return the shipping statement marked "cancel." If I don't cancel, I will receive 4 brand-new novels every month and be billed just $4.24 per book in the U.S., or $4.99 per book in Canada, plus 25¢ shipping and handling per book and applicable taxes, if any*. That's a savings of close to 15% off the cover price! I understand that accepting the 2 free books and gifts places me under no obligation to buy anything. I can always return a shipment and cancel at any time. Even if I never buy another book from Harlequin, the two free books and gifts are mine to keep forever.

154 HDN EEZK   354 HDN EEZV

Name _____ (PLEASE PRINT) _____

Address _____ Apt. # _____

City _____ State/Prov. _____ Zip/Postal Code _____

Signature (if under 18, a parent or guardian must sign) _____

Mail to the **Harlequin Reader Service®**:
IN U.S.A.: P.O. Box 1867, Buffalo, NY 14240-1867
IN CANADA: P.O. Box 609, Fort Erie, Ontario L2A 5X3

Not valid to current Harlequin American Romance subscribers.

Want to try two free books from another line?
Call 1-800-873-8635 or visit www.morefreebooks.com.

* Terms and prices subject to change without notice. NY residents add applicable sales tax. Canadian residents will be charged applicable provincial taxes and GST. This offer is limited to one order per household. All orders subject to approval. Credit or debit balances in a customer's account(s) may be offset by any other outstanding balance owed by or to the customer. Please allow 4 to 6 weeks for delivery.

Your Privacy: Harlequin is committed to protecting your privacy. Our Privacy Policy is available online at www.eHarlequin.com or upon request from the Reader Service. From time to time we make our lists of customers available to reputable firms who may have a product or service of interest to you. If you would prefer we not share your name and address, please check here. ☐

HAR07

Inside ROMANCE

Stay up-to-date on all your
romance reading news!

Inside Romance is a FREE quarterly newsletter
highlighting our upcoming series releases
and promotions.

Visit
www.eHarlequin.com/InsideRomance
to sign up to receive our complimentary newsletter today!

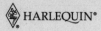